A CRITERION BOOK

FOR YOUNG PEOPLE

THE LOON LAKE MYSTERY
An Alaskan Tale

The Loon Lake Mystery

An Alaskan Tale

by Donnis Thompson

ILLUSTRATED BY RICHARD LEWIS

CRITERION BOOKS, *New York*

Library of Congress Catalog Card Number: 66-15167
Printed in the United States of America

Contents

THE LOON LAKE MYSTERY
An Alaskan Tale

CHAPTER ONE

Todd Comes to Loon Lake

Buff and Todd dashed down to the dock where the canoe was tied. "Now, Todd, since you asked, the way to get into a canoe is to hold onto both sides so you can steady it. Watch me."

With admiring eyes, Todd watched his blond Alaskan cousin climb carefully but effortlessly into the canoe. Then he said, "Now?"

Buff looked up, "Now. You get in the front and we'll both paddle. Easy now," he directed. "Easy. There. Perfect."

In the boat the boys sat so low in the water that Todd could scarcely see above the tall water lilies that grew in profusion about the lake. The lilies had huge yellow blossoms, and, from the canoe, it looked almost as if they were in a jungle – a tropical jungle. Todd took the paddle that

Buff handed him. "I'm afraid I don't know how to use this, Buff, but I sure do want to learn."

"You will, you will. By the time you've been here all summer, you'll be a regular sourdough."

The boys turned as they heard the cabin door open and close. Todd's eager brown eyes were shining. "Hi, Aunt Sally. Look at me!"

Buff waved. "Wanna go, Mom? We can make room. This city slicker in the front seat is a sort of skinny fourteen-year-old. He doesn't take up much space."

For just a moment, a cloud passed over Todd's happy face. Buff's voice had been kind and teasing; but the remark was a bitter reminder to Todd – a reminder that he was always the little one, the skinny one, the last one to finish a race. It was the reason he had begged and pleaded with his father to let him come to Alaska this summer: he felt that maybe, just maybe, he could somehow, way up on a homestead, grow and get some muscles. It all sounded so big, so outdoorish.

Surely, surely, if he tried, if he worked hard, if he stayed outdoors most of the summer, surely, he could get to the place where he could at least *tie* with Jamey. It was just awful to have a brother a year younger than you who could beat you at everything. There was something else, too: at home, everyone really expected him to lose. Why not? He always did, didn't he? They were kind, they were helpful, they told him to keep practicing; but it didn't change things. He always lost and he was sure they always really knew that he would. Up in Alaska, he reasoned, people wouldn't know all that and maybe he could break the habit of losing.

He resolutely shook his head as if to force himself to quit thinking unhappy thoughts. Besides, it wasn't so bad being called skinny by a big, fifteen-year-old Alaskan who was as nice as Buff.

He turned to watch Aunt Sally, who was walking down the path from the cabin. She wore blue jeans and a red cotton flannel shirt. As she came onto the dock, she smiled at them. "No, I don't want to go," she said, "but it is a lovely evening. Have a good time, boys. And Buff, don't wear Todd out on his first day here. Maybe you should be back in a couple of hours or so."

Todd had never seen a woman who looked quite like Aunt Sally. Back in the city, women didn't dress that way. And something else was different; maybe it was her hair – all blowy. He guessed she didn't bother with it very much. But she was pretty. Her face looked sunny, and she smiled often. He knew from the letters the families had written back and forth that Aunt Sally had shot several moose and helped butcher them. Todd felt a sudden loyalty to this aunt he had just met. Maybe she isn't as stylish as women in the city, he thought; but then, none of them probably ever skinned a moose either.

Buff gently pushed the canoe away from the dock. "Todd, see this path ahead in the water? We made it by diving down and pulling out lilies by their roots. We'll head down the path and, in just a few yards, we'll be past the lilies and then we can see where we're going, and you can decide what part of the lake you want to explore."

"What part? Oh, I want to explore all of it. How do I steer with this paddle?"

"Don't worry about that. Just paddle. I can guide us from back here."

The canoe began to glide down the lily-lined "path." There was a gentle swish in the water. Todd looked about as they came to the end of the path and onto the main part of the lake. The late rays of sun were playing on the still, clear water. Tips of tall spruce and an occasional birch and cottonwood that leaned out over the lake were casting their reflections in nature's mirror. From one edge of the lake, grebes were giving their chattering calls. As he watched, two ducks swam silently through the lilies. "Oh, my!" he breathed.

They paddled to the other side of the lake, then poked about the banks looking at fallen trees in the water and watching fish dart like black shadows beneath them. The cabin was built on a bit of land that jutted into the lake and this peninsula made it seem like two lakes; so when the boys had worked around one lake, they went through the small channel, past the cabin, and on to the bigger body of water. It was almost a mile to the end of this lake and it took some hard paddling to get there. Upon reaching the bank, they got out and pulled the canoe up on the shore. Standing in the wet weeds, they watched a shore bird bob about on a little sandy point of beach. A shallow but wide stream ran from this end of the lake for several miles out to Cook Inlet, which was salt water and an arm of the Pacific Ocean.

A couple of enormous beaver houses and a beaver dam were there and the dam had formed a little pool in the stream. Buff told Todd that it was a continuing battle between the beavers and his family to keep the dam the way

each side wanted it. The beavers would work and work on it, and soon the whole level of the lake would rise a bit. Buff or his father would tear some of it out to let the water escape and, in season, to let the salmon get up the stream and on into the lake.

Buff pulled a handful of green grass and tasted a bit of it. He offered some to Todd. "Isn't it just a weed?" But Todd chewed the blades of grass and found them salty, and not unpleasant.

"Goose tongue," Buff told him. "It makes good greens." He took another weed and showed Todd that it was hollow and came apart in neat little sections. "Joint grass. See, you could use it for straws."

The boys sat down on the bank and began idly playing with the joint grass, pulling it apart, looking at the sky, glancing at the lake. Buff said that if they were quiet they might see a beaver. Todd waited, keeping very still.

Suddenly, his attention was diverted by something he saw floating in the water, backed close to the bank by a small eddy. He swooped down, reached out, and retrieved it. It was a small wooden thing that had a hole running through it longways. It was evidently old, for most of the bright paint was peeling off, showing the worn wood underneath. It was shaped about like a football and was about the size of two oranges fastened together.

He turned to show it to Buff. "What is this?"

Buff looked at it. "Why, it's a float off a cork line. Where did you get it?"

"Right here in the water. What's it for?"

"Oh, it goes on a commercial fishing net. They have this

big long net, and one side has a lead line or some weights running along it to sink it, and the other side has these floats that hold that side up so that the net is stretched out to catch the fish. But what would it be doing way back here? How on earth did it get here?" He examined it thoughtfully and frowned intently. "I can't understand it."

"Someone must have dropped it."

"Who? There isn't any *someone* around here."

"What do you mean? Not *anybody?*" He gazed in sudden realization at the woods around him.

"That's right. Not anybody. We have the Jacksons for neighbors back down our road. You remember, we passed the place about three miles before we got home? But in this other direction, it's still government land, so no one lives there."

"You call someone who lives three miles away a neighbor?"

"Up here, they are." He indicated the float. "Besides, this isn't something you just carry around with you."

"Well, *I* don't, anyway," Todd agreed.

"And it's miles to the fishing water."

"Very good point. But what do you mean?"

"Well, the only ones who would be using this kind of a thing would be commercial fishermen, and the only place they can fish legally is out on the Inlet, either in boats or on beach sites, and it's just miles to the beach."

Todd sighed. "I'm not going to guess anymore. Nobody could have dropped that thing, because nobody lives here. Boy, I'll bet Sherlock Holmes would have a terrific time in Alaska. The butler could never be a suspect."

Buff laughed. "You're crazy, or maybe we both are. Anyway, I'm going to take this back with me and show it to Mom and then to Dad when he comes home this weekend."

"Is it really that mysterious?"

Buff shrugged. "In a way, yes. I guess it's not serious, but I just can't understand it."

Buff tossed it in the canoe and it just lay there innocently. There was no sudden chill in the air. There was no blare of bugles. There was no warning, no way for the boys to know that, in just three days, they would be led down an avenue of terror, and all because Todd found that float.

They got back into the canoe and shoved off. As they settled down to steady paddling, Buff asked, "Well, Todd, what do you think of our lake?"

"Are you kidding? I think you're the luckiest guy alive. How come your dad, instead of mine, had to be the adventurer in the family and come to Alaska to live?"

The boys continued their idle talk, then Todd turned the canoe and headed toward the cabin. A wisp of smoke came from the chimney, showing that Aunt Sally had already felt the evening chill that crept into the cabin even in June. As the canoe pulled to a halt, Todd gazed a moment at the house nestled between the trees and the thin spiral of smoke rising among the spruce. It's like something out of a storybook, he thought. Then he climbed out. He showed his red, blistered hands to Buff. "I guess," he said ruefully, "I'm anything but a sourdough. Isn't that what you said I'd be?"

"Yes, but give yourself time. You'll toughen up in a hurry.

Shall we go in and get something to eat before we go to bed? It's getting late, and we have lots to do tomorrow."

Todd looked bewildered. "I don't know. I'm so mixed up about the time. Have we had dinner? How late is it? It's still light."

"Yes, we've had supper – or dinner, as you say. I know you get mixed up on the time changes when you fly. But it's almost eleven."

"It can't be. The sun's still up."

"I've got news for you: it hardly goes down at all in the summer." He turned and pointed at the red rays sparkling through the sharp spires of spruce. "See, it doesn't get much darker, then it starts getting lighter again."

"I guess I knew that, too, but I had forgotten it. Sure seems sunny, doesn't it?"

"No," Buff said. "I've never known it any other way. I like it and it seems we can get so much done. We go like crazy all summer long, 'cause in winter it's just as dark as it is light in summer."

"Okay, you Alaskan. I guess I'm like the rooster that thought that it was just his crowing that brought the sun up in the east every morning. I guess if you're not used to it getting dark, it wouldn't seem funny – what's the matter with you?"

Buff was doubled over laughing. "I didn't know things were so different. That old rooster would have a time up here."

"Why?"

" 'Cause the sun doesn't really come up in the east here."

"Oh, come on, now. I may be in Alaska, but I'm not on Mars. You can't change the course of the sun."

"That's right. But look at that sun now. It's not going down in the west. That's north."

"You mean it? The sun goes down in the north and comes up in the south?"

"That's closer than east and west is. We'll take a look at a globe someday and I'll show you." Buff looked at his cousin. "Come on, you can digest it all some other time this summer. You've had enough changes for today. I'll give you something substantial to digest and one more change. Let's go in and get a great big moose roast sandwich before we go to bed."

"You mean that wasn't beef we ate for dinner, or supper, or whatever it was we ate up in this crazy country?"

"Yep. And I win a bet. I have a standing bet with Mom on which company will notice that it isn't beef. She likes beef better and says she can tell the difference, but I win most of the bets."

The boys stored the life jackets on the back porch and went into the neat cabin. "Hi, Mom," Buff said as he took some water from the teakettle and poured it into a washbasin, so they could clean up.

"Hello, boys. It's about time you came in. Getting pretty late. Todd, how did it go? Did he wear you out on your first evening? He's been so eager for company, he'll probably want to show you everything at once."

"I don't know that Buff wore me out, but the canoe paddles did a pretty good job. I'm real soft."

"If you boys want something to eat, hop to it. Tomorrow

we've got a lot of work to do. When Dad comes back this weekend, we want to show some real progress."

"You just line up the jobs, Mom. I've got good help here now. Only, just give us a chance to get in a little fishing. Todd's got to have a whopper of a tale for the city folks back home." When Buff said that, he had no idea how big a whopper Todd would have; and since he didn't know, he didn't worry. He just bit off a huge chunk of roast moose and grinned at Todd who was doing likewise.

CHAPTER TWO

A City Boy Gets Acquainted

Todd opened his eyes quickly, questioningly, trying to remember where he was. A shaft of bright, hard sunshine was coming in at the edge of the curtain where it had not been pulled over far enough. He was not in the apartment where the sounds of traffic in the streets below provided a constant muted hum he was used to, where even the screeching sirens were blended with the other noises so that he scarcely noticed them. *There* – that noise! That was what woke him up. What could it be? It started as a loud, shrill, but somehow melodic scream, then it broke and ran up and down the scale, full of trills. Then a full chorus joined it: cackles, yells, whistles. It all went on and on.

He turned a bit on his bunk and looked around. There were four built-in beds in the bunk room, though only two of them were occupied, his and Buff's. As Buff explained it, they were equipped to put up lots of people if they needed to, whether for emergency or pleasure. Buff's mother and father had a separate bedroom. Along one wall of the boys' room were shelves and a couple of dressers and, above them, treasures supplied by Buff: a small moose rack of horns, from which he hung his watch, a string tie, belts, and other odd possessions; and a stuffed ptarmigan staring across the moose rack at a stuffed spruce hen. On top of one of the dressers was a beaver skeleton with its big teeth permanently gnashing. Todd couldn't decide whether he appreciated this type of decoration or not. For one silly second, he tried to picture it back in the elegant apartment at home, maybe right on top of the huge slab of marble that was a coffee table. He thought of his parents' friends. I wonder, he mused, if I sneaked it in and they were told it was a famous piece of sculpture by a famous person, what they would say about it? He almost laughed, but caught himself.

He was bone-tired but he couldn't sleep. He couldn't really believe yet that he was actually in Alaska. You could fly so fast and so far in a jet these days that you just couldn't catch up mentally. That eternal racket was still going on outside, and behind the general mayhem, was the flutelike trill of *something,* moving up and down the scale, then starting all over again. I'll bet if you heard that on a dark night it would bring frightening chills, he thought. He looked at Buff who was not stirring. How *do* they sleep through it all? It must be awfully late.

As silently as possible, he slipped out of the bunk room,

through the living room, and onto the screened-in porch. The sun was high, and blindingly bright. He stretched, and felt his muscles grab from the canoeing. He wondered what time these supposedly rugged Alaskans got up. He had presumed it was like on a farm: up at daybreak. At least that was the way his father had represented it to him.

He thought of his father and sighed. His father had played first string on the college football team and had broken all kinds of records in his high school track days – records that still held. Todd remembered being taken on a tour of that high school one day and the trophies his father had won were proudly pointed out to him. They winked and blinked at him from their cases and seemed, to him, as unattainable as lollipops on Venus.

But that wasn't the worst. Oh, by no means, that wasn't the worst. The worst was his brother Jamey, who was a year younger than Todd and a good two inches taller already, and a full eon ahead of him in muscle, in prowess, in accomplishments, in everything. To get it from both directions was murder: a younger brother who could lick you and a father who must be disappointed in you.

As the old troubles swept through him, Todd opened the screen door and sat down on the top step. The lake was before him, and from one corner came one racket, from another corner another racket. The birds had divided up the lake. A smile crossed his lips and he thought of a song they used to sing in Sunday school, "You in your small corner, and I in mine."

As he watched, small fish jumped from the lake. Splat,

splat, here a splat, there a splat. That reminded him of another song. He watched the fish intently, then realized he was not alone. Suddenly, a bird – *some* kind of bird – soared, rose, circled, then dived with the swift intensity of a bomber. There was a small flurry on the lake as the bird made contact, and then the universe was suddenly over for one fish. Todd could see the outline of the catch in the bird's beak as it flew away. He sucked in his breath at the drama he had witnessed. Better than TV any day. It was so *real,* this life-and-death struggle, it gave him the goose bumps.

He happened to glance down at his watch. It said four-thirty. He stared at it in disbelief, then shook it. It must have stopped. No, the second hand was still running. Then it dawned on him. Buff had said it didn't get dark. It probably was four-thirty. No wonder no one else was up. "Well, whadya know?" he said lightly under his breath. "I'll never get used to this country."

He crept back into the darkened bunk room, and glanced more appreciatively at the heavy drapes. He adjusted the one to keep out the small line of sunshine, then plopped back into bed. His last thought before going back to sleep was, Just the same, I'm glad I woke up. I'm glad I saw the lake all by myself. We never seem to do anything *alone* in cities.

It was sometime later that he groggily heard Aunt Sally say to Buff, "Oh, let's let him sleep until he wakes up. He's had a big trip and he's tired. Besides, remember, when you travel the change in time is confusing. Back at his home, it would only be two in the morning."

Todd shook his head to get awake, then called, "You don't know the half of it – how mixed up I am." He staggered from bed and pulled on his shirt and jeans.

Buff laughed. "Let's go wash our faces in the lake. That'll wake you up." They dashed out and walked out on the dock. Todd caught sight of a V in the water. At the head of it was a tiny face, and at the back a hairless little tail following like a rudder. "What is it?" he whispered hoarsely to Buff.

"It's a muskrat. We've lots of them. You'll see them all the time."

As the shock of the cold lake water sent the blood tingling through Todd, he asked Buff, "How do you ever get anything done here? Every time I look at the lake, there's something different to see."

Buff answered dryly. "That's one of my problems, too, and as long as I've lived here, I haven't solved it. To hear my folks tell it, I probably won't." But he grinned as he spoke.

Todd wiped his face on the towel Buff provided, and he pulled his comb from his pants pocket and used it. The warm sun had a hypnotic effect until the smell of bacon and coffee began filling the air. Todd sniffed. "Wow! That's the best smell I ever smelled!"

"Let's race." Buff tore off, leaving Todd behind, but then Todd was used to that, and besides, he was still stiff and sore.

As they started in on Aunt Sally's man-sized breakfast, Todd said, "I know I'm not a sourdough. What do you call someone that isn't?"

"You're a cheechako."

"Cheechako? That's a great-sounding name. I think I'll write Mom and Dad that I'm a cheechako and they'll never know but what it's something terrific."

Aunt Sally smiled. "I think I'll wait until the end of the summer and tell them you're a sourdough. That might be terrific-er."

Todd smiled back at her. But a worry was forming in the back of his mind. They didn't know his reputation for coming in last and he didn't want to disappoint them too. Was it as hard to become a sourdough as to make a touchdown? He crossed his fingers under the table.

While they ate breakfast, Aunt Sally and Buff told Todd about the projects they were working on, but he didn't understand a word of it. Back home, a job was usually an errand to run. Evidently that wasn't true on a homestead.

"One big thing we've just got to take care of is a new well. The other ran dry last fall, and we've been using lake water ever since. Your Uncle David tried to put down a well point the last two or three weekends, but we always had some kind of trouble. Now that school's out, maybe Buff and you can get that done. If we run out of parts, I can drive to town. The road was pretty good yesterday when we went to meet your plane. I don't know. It's a problem. Would it be better to try to dig the well we've got deeper or just drive a new well point down? If we start a new one, it won't be in our back porch – unless we tear up the floor in the porch. I don't know. . . ."

Todd was trying hard to follow Aunt Sally's ramblings. But what on earth was she talking about? He helped himself to another of her sourdough pancakes and tried to decide again whether he really liked them or not. Such a peculiar taste.

Buff looked up. "Hey, Todd, have you tried this rose-hip jelly?" He indicated a jar of delicate pink.

"Thanks. Rose what?"

"Rose hips. You know the center part that's left from the wild roses after the petals fall off. We make jelly out of them. Better than oranges for vitamin C."

Todd looked uncertainly at Aunt Sally. He had heard of the jokes and pranks that Alaskans liked to pull on the newcomers.

But Aunt Sally smiled. "He's right. Try it. You'll like it. Then, if we get the well finished, or if we decide we can't get the well finished, we've *got* to get the roots and underbrush cleaned out in the clearing. The Jacksons will be here to cultivate in no time."

Buff grinned and winked at Todd. He was used to his mother's switching from one subject to another without pausing for breath.

After much discussion, it was decided to let the well go, at least for a bit. The boys carried buckets of water, dipping them from the lake, and Aunt Sally took a white cloth and strained the water to get any dirt or sticks out of it.

Todd stared. "Do you mean we are drinking that lake water? Do you boil it?"

"No, we don't. There's no chance of pollution up here. There's no one on the lake, nor anyone within miles. It's safe up here."

Aunt Sally smiled. "I know how you feel, Todd. I don't

drink much of it. I make coffee out of mine and that way it's boiled. Don't worry, though. We wouldn't think of drinking from a lake out in your country either."

Todd hated to tell them what was bothering him. Maybe they were right about the germs, maybe it was perfectly safe; but just the same, he had seen muskrats, fish, and birds in that water. Maybe he was drinking water that something had just swished through. How long did it take for that particular amount of water to be sterilized? He made a mental note to try to drink coffee for the next few days until he and Buff could drive that well. He wondered idly, How in the world do you *drive* a well point?

After the water was in, they cut firewood and filled up the box just in case of an evening chill. Then, when Todd was thinking he had just put in more physical work than he could ever remember doing before, Buff said, "Well, shall we get started?"

"Started? I thought we were just about finished."

"Those were just the chores. Now, we go to the field."

With hatchets, an ax, and a canteen, they walked up the drive to the clearing. Todd was careful to carry his ax on the shoulder that wasn't sore from paddling. The work at the clearing was extremely simple: they chopped, and cut, and dug, and then they pulled the stumps and roots and brush in the field. The sun came down, and the mosquitoes came out. Streams of sweat poured from Todd and the smashed mosquitoes just sort of swam in it. Buff pulled a can of spray repellent from his pocket and used it on them both, making them sneeze and cough. But the mosquitoes kept at a distance.

As they both got to the brush pile together once with a load, Buff said, "I think you're getting the hang of it."

Gamely, but wearily, Todd said, "I *understand* it, all right; it's *doing* it that gives me trouble."

After what Todd judged to be about thirty days and thirty nights of unrelieved slavery, they heard a horn and Buff yelled, "It's dinnertime!"

Almost in a daze, Todd staggered through the field and down the drive to the house with Buff. They put their tools on the back porch and Buff yelled, "Hey, Mom! Have we got time for a five-minute swim?"

"Five and a half."

Quickly the boys put on trunks, dashed down to the dock, and Buff dived in. Todd stepped off one end gingerly. Holy cow, but that was cold! A minute ago, he hadn't thought he'd ever be cool again and he had been mentally composing letters back home telling the folks how they had this Alaska all wrong. His foot settled down into some deep oozy silt which struck him as being unpleasant, so he held his breath and plunged. He swam out near Buff, who had gone to a floating dock. Buff said, "Well, I'm cooled off. We never stay in very long."

Goose pimples were running up and down Todd. "Wise decision. Wi-ise decision. I think I just sideswiped an ice cube anyway."

But they felt warm, clean, and fine when they dried off. Aunt Sally had soup and huge sandwiches ready for them. Todd ate more than he could ever remember eating before in his life. He marveled again at the canned butter, which was a staple, he was told. He tried to hide his dislike for the powdered milk, which they also said was all they ever used. He asked for the rose-hip jelly like an old-timer. Full of food, tired, and warm after the swim, he began to get drowsy right at the table.

Aunt Sally suggested wisely, "Why don't we all take a nap?"

Todd sat bolt upright. "A nap?" Why, naps were for babies and old people. "Oh, no," he said sleepily. "I'm okay. Why, if we take a nap, we'll be late for work."

"Late? What's late? We don't quit at five o'clock. If you want to, you can work all night up here."

Todd thought a minute. "Yes, I guess you can. Gee, it seems kind of funny that you don't need a schedule. Why is it that things have to be done by a certain time back home? I've sort of forgotten."

"I'll tell you what," Aunt Sally said, "I'll clear up the table and you boys take a nap. Why don't you go lie right on the dock? The sun's so nice and warm today, it's a shame to waste it; and I think there's enough of a breeze off the lake, so the mosquitoes shouldn't be too bad."

After a short sunny nap on the dock, the boys started back to the field, but Aunt Sally stopped them. "Let's not work Todd too hard right away. I know you really accomplished a lot this morning. Just work a couple of hours this afternoon, then knock off for a while, take a boat ride, or whatever you want to do, and there'll only be one more job for the day."

"Is this a trap, Mom?"

"No, indeed. The job is to supply us with enough trout for supper on your boat ride."

"It's a deal."

Later, finished with the day's work, they piled fishing equipment, binoculars, and life jackets into the boat. They rowed out into the lake, picked a likely-looking spot, and tossed their lines out. Todd was given a spinning rod and they put a small lure on it – a red and white spoon. Buff said he guessed he'd be lazy and different, so he used some single salmon eggs on the end of a hook and dropped his line in. Todd wrinkled up his nose. "Whoo-ee, but those smell awful."

Buff grinned. "Practically the next thing to caviar. Don't you have any class?" After he dropped his line in, he gave Todd some instructions on how to use his rig, and how to reel it in to get the proper spoon action.

The sun slanted down and a small breeze played across the water, rustling the huge leaves of the water lilies. That crazy, shrill cry sounded from the end of the lake, echoed back from the hillside, and then was joined by a terrific quacking from the other end of the lake.

"What makes that noise? I heard it early this morning."

"The one that goes up and down the scale, sort of, is a loon. We have a pair that nest here every year. During parts of the summer, they swim out across the lake a couple of times a day. Real neighborly. But when they are busy with nesting, we don't see much of them. The rest of the racket is mostly from the grebes. Sometimes we hear the ducks, but they mostly make a quack that you can recognize. The grebes might look a little like a duck to you, but they're different. They have a skinny, sort of

reddish neck. There's a bunch of them that hang out in that one corner of the lake, back in the lily pads."

"Crazy as a loon," Todd murmured. "I see where that expression comes from now. I kind of like it, even if it is creepy sometimes."

"One nice thing, though: most of the time that you hear the loons up here, it's pretty light, and the ghosts can't get you."

Todd grinned, and wrinkled up his nose at Buff, then gasped suddenly.

"B-b-bish, I got a fuf – I mean, I mean, Buff, wha'do, I do now? Quick! I got a fish!" His hands were shaking.

Buff said, "Well, the first thing is to sit still or we're both going to be right in the lake with him. Take it easy, take it easy. Did he really take it? Is he on?" For an answer, the fish boiled to the surface and flounced and splashed. "Okay, okay! He looks hooked, all right. Just let him play a bit; keep your line tight. Try to keep him on your side of the boat. You can start reeling in slowly."

Todd tried very hard to follow every one of Buff's instructions, but it did seem to him that Buff didn't understand the urgency of the situation. He had a fish on! A real, true fish was fighting, splashing, feinting, whamming on the line.

"He must be a monster! Gee whiz, I'll bet he weighs twenty pounds!"

He couldn't see Buff's amused and slightly puzzled look. Finally, the fish was alongside and Buff started to reach out to help, then shook his head. "No, I guess I won't. I'll let you get him a hundred per cent. Either give him a little flip in, or hold the pole in your right hand and reach down with your left and grab him."

Todd held the pole, then reached down to where the fish was still splashing a bit. "Grab him?"

"Sure. Just take hold of him."

Wherever Todd seemed to reach, the fish just then, wasn't. When he did manage to touch him, the slick and slimy fish scooted just out of his hand, and frothed the lake again, throwing splashes in Todd's face. Todd instinctively reared back. Finally he grabbed, and when he made contact, he squeezed. With a flip, the fish was safely in the boat.

"I did it! I did it! I landed him! I did it all by myself, didn't I? I mean, really; really and truly."

Buff said, "You did it all by yourself, really and truly." He wondered about Todd. Hadn't he ever caught a fish before? "Yep. That's a dandy. Must be about fifteen inches long."

"How much does he weigh?"

"Oh, I don't know. I suppose a pound and a half."

"A pound and a half? Why, I thought it would weigh at least twenty." He marveled. "If that was a pound-and-a-half fish, what must it be to catch a twenty-pounder? What kind is it?"

"It's a rainbow trout."

Todd sounded as if he were memorizing. "It was a rainbow trout. It was fifteen inches long, and it weighed a pound and a half, and I caught it."

"Don't quote me on all that. It's just an estimate. Well, we need a few more if we're going to have enough to eat for supper."

"Eat it? We're going to eat it? Well, yes, I guess we are." He leaned back, exhausted. "Do you mean we've got to go through all that again?"

Buff laughed. "Well, not if the fish won't cooperate."

But the fish cooperated fine. Buff caught three and Todd caught another one. This one didn't give him quite as much thrill, but then for the rest of his whole life there would never be another like the first one. He felt he was an old pro by now. The wind was coming up stronger, the sun had gone under, and Todd found out how thin was the margin in Alaska between summer weather and cool weather. One minute he was comfortable, and the next, he was getting downright cold.

The canoe began riding little swells. "Let's get home, okay?" Buff said, as he commenced paddling.

The lake was a little over a mile in length and they were about midway in it. The wind blew harder and colder. After several minutes of hard paddling with little progress, Todd yelled back over his shoulder, "How fast do you figure we're going backward?" As he put his head into the wind, and paddled with hard, quick, though still awkward strokes, he felt the heady exultation of pitting his strength against the elements. Though tears were streaming from his eyes from the wind, he let out a wild yell followed by a triumphant laugh. More power than he knew he had seemed to charge through his tired, aching arms. It was a thrill he had never experienced before. They rounded the bend, sent the bow of the canoe down the lily path and alongside the dock.

Buff slapped Todd on the back. "Some boat ride, huh? Say, you're really doin' all right on that paddle." He began unloading things quickly, but Todd just stood for a minute, savoring every minute of the sensation of the challenge, the conquering of it; and, at the end, a partner saying, "Well done."

As Buff was gathering equipment from the canoe, he spied the float. He picked it up gingerly, wonderingly, with a frown on his face. "I can't understand it."

Todd had forgotten all about it. "Oh, that thing. That's right. You said it was mysterious."

"The float isn't mysterious, but how in the world it ever got there, is."

"I don't see why. Everything's mysterious in this country. The sun comes up in the wrong direction, never does remember to go down; people drink lake water, make jelly out of flowers –"

He was interrupted by Aunt Sally who called that she was popping the biscuits in the oven and heating the skillets for the fish. Quickly, the boys went down the lake a little way and cleaned the trout, Buff doing most of the work. Todd tried hard to remember which one was his, and tried to memorize the size and shape of at least one fillet; but they all looked dismayingly alike. He was ashamed to admit to Buff that he would have liked to keep his fish separate.

The three of them sat at the table, looking out over the lake. The wind continued to blow. It whistled about the cabin, and gave an eerie and completely different look to the lake. The choppy waves looked boiling and dirty. Some terns – aristocratic and graceful – whirled, dived, rose, and rode on the wind over the lake. Todd said quietly, "You know, I think that's the most elegant bird I ever saw."

Buff nodded in agreement. "Yes, they are. Mean, though. Boy, are they mean! They'll take out after birds several times their size. Nasty temper, but beautiful."

Aunt Sally said appreciatively, "This trout is wonderful. It tastes so much better when you catch it like this and pop it right in the skillet than when you buy it in the store. Don't you think so, Todd?"

"I don't think we ever bought rainbows in the store, but it's sure good."

Buff contributed generously, "I think Todd's is the best, too. Did you know he caught two, Mom?"

Todd looked up, astonished. "Mine is the best? How can you tell? They all looked alike to me."

"Oh, I noticed when we were cleaning them that one of yours had a little pinkish cast to the meat."

"Pinkish cast?" He dug into his trout to inspect it.

"Sure. Here, if you haven't tried it, here's another piece of it."

Eagerly, Todd tried it. "Oh, it is good, isn't it? It's a lot better. I wonder why it's so much better?" Happily, he salted it and ate it with bread and butter. The world was truly good. He had caught the very best fish. He did not see Buff wink at his mother.

That evening the breeze continued and they stayed inside and built a fire in the wood stove. The stove was a common type on Alaska homesteads. It had been made from an oil barrel that was turned on its side, legs attached to it, and a door cut in the top of the barrel which was now the front of the stove. They had a flat sheet of metal welded to the top so they could cook on it, and it always held a handy teakettle of hot water. The fire seemed cozy and they lazily watched the evening close in. It was almost a real, honest-to-goodness dark evening now because of the winds and dark clouds.

Buff started a popper of popcorn and turned to Todd. "Now, tell me about the big city. I've been showing you birds and lakes and canoes. . . ."

Todd interjected, "Don't forget the ax and the roots and stumps. But fair enough. What would you like to know about?" It was inconceivable to him right then that there would be *anything* a boy like Buff would care to know about a city. A city was so, well, so normal.

But Buff evidently didn't see it that way and, before he knew it, in response to Buff's questioning, Todd was explaining about zoos, throughways, museums, tennis courts, and bus tokens. He was telling how close he lived to school and his father's club where he sometimes went swimming.

"Imagine that," marveled Buff. "I've never been in an indoor swimming pool in my life. It would be nice, just once, to swim in warm water."

The popcorn stopped sputtering and exploding and Buff slid the lid back on the old-fashioned popper and dumped the contents into a bowl, then poured melted butter on it, some salt, and passed the bowl to Todd.

Aunt Sally joined them, and she asked questions about Todd's folks whom she hadn't seen in a long time. They discussed the advantages of living close to school and stores. "Yes," Buff said, "you don't know what it's like to walk four miles to catch the bus and ride on it for forty minutes to school. It's cold and it's dark when I leave and it's dark when I get home. When I try to go out for basketball or a play, or *anything,* I have a miserable time getting home. I try to catch a ride with someone coming out this way. Sometimes, I stay overnight with a friend, but I can't just camp there. Everyone up here has a small house and basketball practice goes on every night in the week. When I was in grade school, I took correspondence courses. Lots of kids in Alaska who live in the bush do that. But when I got to high school, the folks thought I was old enough to go back and forth, and I wanted some of the extras: sports, and the science classes with a laboratory, and seeing other kids – you know. But all the traveling sure gets tiresome."

"I can see that all right. But it would be worth it. You can be outdoors. When you get home, there's something interesting going on all the time. Not just a kind of fancy apartment where you always have to be careful of things. Besides, what's so hot about basketball?"

"Well, I like it. We don't have many sports up here. Don't you play?"

Todd laughed a bit grimly. "Oh, sure, I go out, but that's all. We've got five thousand kids in our school. 'Course, Jamey plays on his class team."

Buff looked at his mother and they both reflected their concern at Todd's tone. Aunt Sally said, "Yes, well, up here, they are lucky if they have a full string of substitutes on the team. I guess it's different, all right, and each way has its drawbacks and problems."

The pleasant, relaxed evening wore on and Buff was in bed and almost alseep when he suddenly remembered that he had not told his mother about the float Todd had found. Wondering again how the float happened to be there, he drifted off to sleep.

CHAPTER THREE

Water and a Strange Noise

In the morning, Aunt Sally announced that she was going into town. "I want to see if there's a letter from Dad. I'll take the radio in and have them look at it and see what's wrong. Maybe it's something simple. I'll stop at Jackson's and see when they plan to come here to cultivate. How far along are you on the field clearing, boys?"

"Let's face it," Buff said. "It won't be perfect for another twenty years, but the big stuff is coming along. Jackson can't come in and treat it like an Iowa farm, but if he's careful, he shouldn't tear up too much equipment."

"That's fine," she said dryly. "All we need is a bill for Jackson's machinery that our field wrecks."

"Maybe you should sign a contract in advance and state who's liable for what," Todd suggested.

Aunt Sally stared at him. "You're a pretty bright boy. We just never seem to get around to doing things right up here. But in the first place, it would probably make Mr. Jackson mad if we asked him to actually sign anything, but maybe we can come to some sort of an agreement beforehand. He's an honorable man, after all."

"Well, if he wouldn't sign an agreement, I'd get someone who would."

Buff and his mother exchanged smiles. "There isn't any 'someone else.' We're lucky he'll even bother with us, considering how small our clearing is."

"Small? How big is it? I thought it was the biggest field in the whole world. It sure seems that way when you're trying to get all the brush out."

Aunt Sally's usually sunny face had a frown on it. "Well, it's only about eight acres or so and that's part of the trouble. We've got to get twenty cleared and planted, and I just don't see how – Oh well, those are our troubles. No use worrying you, Todd." She stood up briskly. "Let's plan the day. Let's go and decide on this well. If it looks like we need more pipe or equipment, I'll pick it up in town today."

Todd tried to look intelligent as Buff and his mother discussed the pros and cons of the well problem. "I just don't think going deeper would do any good on this well, Mom. Dad tried that."

"Yes, but I do want the pump in here. Remember, we practically built this porch around it. But if we'd try another one just a few feet away, it might not be any better than the one we have and we'd have to tear up the porch and rebuild it."

"I'll tell you what let's do. Let's go back in the yard, away from the porch, dig a brand-new well, put some pipe in it, dig a trench, and bury the pipe. Then we'll connect it to the pump right here in the porch."

"Will it work?"

"It will work if we hit water okay. We wouldn't have to auger it. We could just dig and put a well point down. We'll have to insulate around the pipe so it won't freeze next winter."

"Okay. Why don't you try it while I'm gone? If there's water, you should hit it in a few hours. Everywhere else, a shallow well is good enough. How much extra pipe shall I bring back?"

The plans and arrangements were all made. Aunt Sally climbed into the battered old jeep. "Anything you want, either of you?"

Todd considered, "Well, I never thought I'd see the day, but I honestly can't think of a thing I want except twenty feet of iron pipe." But he was impressed. He was impressed that Buff shared so importantly in the family's problems and that he was capable of rendering real help.

As his mother was starting the jeep, Buff yelled, "Bring me an ice-cream cone!"

It was an old joke and she smiled and yelled back, "Coming up – next January!"

Todd started to laugh, picturing Aunt Sally trying to drive thirty miles, part of it over the rough, bumpy homestead road, where you could only travel about five miles an hour, holding an ice-cream cone.

"Hey, Mom! If you aren't back by four this evening, it

will mean you're probably stuck and we'll start walking out for you. You'll know we're coming; okay?"

She considered. "That should give me gobs of time. Okay. Four's the deadline."

With a great gnashing and snorting, the bouncing vehicle took off, and the sound soon grew too faint to be heard.

"Would you really just keep walking until you found her? That could be a long way. Could anything happen to her?"

"Of course. If she had car trouble, she could just leave it and walk on home alone. She's done it. But there are moose and bear, and the bears might be kind of hungry and grouchy right now. We'd have to walk out and get the jeep anyway. So this way, Mom'll know she can count on us."

Buff went into the back porch and came back with two shovels. "Here's a way to learn to appreciate an education real fast." He handed one to Todd. "This, sir, is an idiot stick."

Todd accepted it and grinned. "I think this is getting an education. I've heard of ditch digging all my life and now I'll find out what it's all about."

Buff wandered about. "How does this spot look to you?" He dug up a shovel of dirt.

"It looks exactly like all the other spots. Aren't you supposed to wave a peach twig or something over it, to see if it turns or twitches?"

"Sure, you bet. You just get me a peach twig. I guess peaches grow on trees, don't they?"

"Of course they grow on trees, but we don't have many at home. They grow down South more."

"Well, you live down South."

"Okay, you won that one. But we still don't have many peaches. Anyway, maybe a birch would work."

"Dig, man, dig."

So they dug. And they dug. And they dug. The sun and mosquitoes found them again. They sprayed with insect repellent and wiped sweat and pulled off shirts, then undershirts. They took turns digging, and the one at rest could lie on his back and gaze at the sky, or go into the house for glasses of milk. Todd's attention was directed to a different type of bird, one that seemed very curious about what they were doing.

"Buff, look at that bird. What kind is it?"

"Oh, that's a camp robber. Some people call it a whisky-jack. I think the right name is Canada Jay. They're great pets. We'll put some feed out pretty soon and watch him. But there will be more. They come zooming in through the trees and take turns coming up for a bit to store away. Usually they don't eat it. They take it and fly away and then another one flies in for his share."

Todd rushed into the house for a piece of bread. He also found some leftover pancakes. "See if a whisky-jack likes sourdough any better than I do," he muttered.

He spread the pieces of pancake and bread on a log close to where they were working. Sure enough, just as Buff said, the camp robbers began carrying them off in relays. Some birds were cheats and tried to peck up several bits at a time, their beaks acting like a shish-kabob skewer. For this they would get roundly scolded. Some of the group would patiently put up with this, but some would chase the delinquents right off. Some were hesitant and would gaze at Buff and Todd before snatching a piece and tearing off; others were brazen and impatiently waited their turn from a nearby branch and, as soon as the current feeder had flown, they swooped onto the log for their turn.

Todd watched, fascinated. Soon he could even tell one from another. "Why, they're just like people, aren't they? All kinds."

"Yeah. All kinds. Some do their jobs and others just goof off."

With a good-natured laugh, Todd lunged at Buff. "Pretty subtle, aren't you?"

They rolled about on the ground, then Todd scrambled loose. "So I dig. You persuaded me. I dig."

As Todd was digging, Buff suddenly held up his hand. "Listen just a minute." In the distance, they could hear an engine, a powerful engine, straining and throbbing. "Is that Mom coming back? So soon? It doesn't sound like the jeep."

Todd listened awhile. "If it is, she'll be here soon. We didn't hear her car very long this morning after she left."

Buff was puzzled. "It could be the Jacksons – but Mom was going to stop and see them. She wouldn't have sent them on down yet, unless they just had to do the work today or something."

"If it's the Jacksons, they'll be here before too long."

"Right. But I think I'll take a short walk around the bend and see if anyone is on the road. Want to come?"

Todd hesitated. "We-ell." Then he dropped the shovel decisively.

They walked up the road. No car, no vehicle was in sight. They hiked to the clearing, then to the end of the field, then down the road farther. "I don't think it's anything coming in here. They'd have been here by now, and besides, the sound doesn't get any louder down the road."

Todd agreed. "I think the sound's coming from the direction of that end of the lake. It must be someone over there."

"But who? All that area is closed to homesteading. There just isn't anybody. Jackson lives about three miles up there and the hill shuts off any sound from that direction. We just don't *hear* things back here."

"Maybe you don't, but I do." Todd realized, however, that Buff was in no joking mood. "Does it matter, Buff?"

"No-o, I guess not. I can't imagine why it would. I'm just curious. Well, let's get back. I guess we'd better try to hit water before Mom comes home."

But the sound continued, intermittently, all day; it was a persistent nuisance, like a dull headache, distant but audible. Todd marveled that such a little sound in the distance could make such an impression. Why, at home, a sound like that would be lost in the city's noises.

Buff made a note to mention it to his mother when she came home. Maybe the wind was just right and it was coming from a long way off. Maybe there was some new activity he didn't know about. Road building? Clearing? Oil exploration? Funny.

His attention was suddenly directed to the hole he was digging which was about six feet deep now. "Hey, Todd! Look. This ground is wet."

"Is that good?"

"Sure."

"Just what we always wanted: a mud well."

"Well, you didn't expect Old Faithful to blow, did you?"

"Truthfully, yes, something like that."

"It doesn't work that way. Let's go on down a little." As he put his shovel back down, he found a couple of inches in the waterhole. "She's fillin' up already."

The shovelfuls became mostly water, and finally, Buff decided to get a bucket and do some bailing. They were working in mud now, and they rolled up their trouser legs.

"Hey, Buff. We got water. Isn't that what we want?"

"Yes, but we're still in clay. If we go down a little more, we should hit some nice sand and the water should come in faster and cleaner. Then we've got it made."

As the boys sloshed about, digging, heaving buckets of water and mud about, Todd said, "I don't mean to pry and you don't need to answer if you don't want to, but what did Aunt Sally mean this morning about one of your troubles being the extra clearing?"

"Oh, it's okay. Nothing much to it except money. That seems to be a problem we always live with. We have to clear at least twenty acres and we only have eight cleared, and we're running out of time. The government gives us so long to prove up on the homestead; if we don't do it in time, we lose."

"*You lose your homestead?*" Todd stared at Buff, aghast. He looked at the cabin, the lake, the dock. "You could *lose* this?"

"We've lived here long enough, and we've built the cabin. We could get part of the homestead because of the eight acres of clearing, but we couldn't get the whole hundred and sixty unless we clear twenty acres. It has to be cleared, cultivated, and planted. This is our last summer and we don't begin to have enough money to hire the necessary help for the clearing that has to be done. Lots of people don't really ever mean to farm their homestead, they just like some space out in the country and they only clear the land because the government says they have to. But Dad really wants to farm. We wouldn't make much money, but we don't need much. We get a moose and fish and there are always ducks and geese, things like that.

"Then Dad wants to raise potatoes to sell. Probably we'll get some animals when we get some crops: maybe goats and geese, maybe chickens. But we couldn't begin to feed anything now until we can raise some feed for them. Dad says that if we can't get the whole thing, we might as well sell our improvements to someone who could prove up on it, and move closer to town, because he'd have to be working out anyway if he couldn't farm. You can be in the woods up here and still be pretty close to town, the school and all. Of course, it wouldn't be the same. Our lake and all. . . ." His voice trailed off.

Todd sat down, trying to figure this all out. "Well, how much does all this clearing and stuff cost that you need?"

"The clearing costs something like $150 an acre."

"Twelve acres at $150, why that's only $1,800. Why, that's not much. I think my dad makes almost that in a month."

Buff threw out a bucket of mud. "Maybe your dad does, but mine doesn't. Cash is hard to come by on a homestead. That's why he has to go away to find work in the summer, which is also why we want to farm eventually. It's no fun having Dad gone all the time, and jobs aren't as easy to find as they were a few years ago. That big Alaskan pay you hear about went out with the big defense construction jobs. Oh, I guess the pay is better than stateside, but you have to find the job first, and it's no bonanza any more."

Todd picked up a shovel and started his turn. "What *do* people do up here for a living?"

"Different things. There are a lot of government jobs, all the agencies – like the wildlife control, the aviation, the courts, schools – that kind of thing. There aren't that many oil jobs any more but anyway you have to be where they are and a lot of experienced workers came up from the states and filled most of them. The old-timers mined, and trapped, and fished. The mining is not so hot, the trapping is not so hot, but some years the fishing is still real good. Some years, it isn't, and there never are the big catches there used to be; but still, if you hit it lucky, you could make thousands and thousands of dollars in a real short time. You know, Todd, I told you about it yesterday when we found that float." He frowned, then smiled. "The strangest things start happening when you land on a homestead."

But Todd was hardly listening now. He was thinking of Buff's problems. Maybe, he told himself, everyone has a problem. We just walk around in life talking to people and being with them, and we still don't know how many worries they have. He jabbed his shovel down. Even so, he thought fiercely, I'd rather have Buff's problem than mine. At least he's important. He can help out. Even digging a well helps. There isn't *anything* helpful I can do at home.

Buff examined the last shovelful. "Sand. Good. She's coming out pretty strong, too, isn't she? It should clear up in no time."

Todd looked appreciatively at the hole in the ground and found himself saying, in the proper vernacular, "She looks great."

The boys took a quick swim to wash off some mud, fixed some lunch, then went back to inspect the well. "It looks fine. Let's drive this sand point down, hook up what pipe we have, and hope Mom remembers to bring more." They struggled with things Todd had never used before: wrenches, pipe, fittings. After the initial fitting, Todd was put to work digging a ditch to bury the pipe that was to run from the well to the pump on the porch.

It was almost three when Aunt Sally got back. The jeep came to a stop with a great dusty roar. "Hi, boys! Do we have a well?"

They helped her unload the pipe, the groceries, and various supplies. She was elated with the well and asked them if they had time to eat some rolls and have a conference. "And read the mail. Letters for all of us. You too, Todd."

She made some coffee and put out the rolls she had bought at the store in town. "Here are a couple of cans of pop for you boys. I wrapped a piece of insulation around them. Hope they're still cold."

She handed Todd his letter from home and he stared at the postmark. It brought a surge of homesickness that amazed him. Then he read, in his mother's careful handwriting, a full account of everyday happenings. Although he had only been gone a couple of days when she wrote it it sounded like a message from another world. She complained of the laundry's poor service, told of the morning lecture she had attended, the dinner party she was planning, and the play they had seen the night before. Jamey was spending a lot of time improving his tennis game and doing a lot of swimming. His father added a brief, hurried note for him to "have fun" and added, "Jamey is really developing a hard slamming forehand." Todd closed his eyes and pictured his father – so happy to have a boy with a hard slamming forehand to brag about. Feeling independent and tired from honest, heavy work, however, Todd didn't feel so bad. Gosh, he thought, he just ought to see my mud-slinging forearm. Somehow digging a well seemed more important than tennis right then.

Todd had been so engrossed in his own letter, he was unaware of what Buff and Aunt Sally were discussing so earnestly, until Buff said, "Sure we can. Don't you think so, Todd?"

Aunt Sally helped him out. "I have a letter from Buff's father. He thinks he's got a good job lined up, but it's about three hundred miles away. He wants me to meet him in Anchorage with some clothes and camp things he needs and drive him up to where the job is. I would probably be gone a week."

"We can run the ranch, can't we?"

"Why, I guess so. I'll be glad to try and help. I don't know what to do, but as long as Buff points out which shovel, I'll take it and dig."

Aunt Sally laughed. "It's a good thing you're here, Todd. I

wouldn't think of going otherwise. There's so much work to be done. Oh yes, I stopped in and saw the Jacksons, and they will be here in three or four days. So I got the seed when I was in town. You boys will have to spread it. It will be a big job, because you won't even have the jeep. Try to get it as even as you can. Maybe you should sack it up into small batches beforehand. You'll just have to do the best you can. We never know when an inspector from the land office will show up."

"I remember a picture in the third grade of some Egyptians sprinkling seed. It was a few thousand years ago, but I suppose some things never change."

Buff grinned at Todd. "You know, you look at the world crazy. I don't know whether it's you or your city upbringing."

Aunt Sally jumped up. "Whatever it is, we're glad to have you here. I wouldn't think of leaving Buff here for a week alone. Too many things could happen. Now, let's get as much lined up as we can."

"When do you leave, Aunt Sally?"

"We're to listen to Mukluk. Tonight or tomorrow we'll get a message and find out for sure. It's a good thing I took the radio in and got it fixed."

Todd looked puzzled. "What in the world does that mean? I thought a mukluk was an Eskimo shoe. My, what customs you have! Messages from shoes! Do you read tea leaves, too?"

Buff explained. "That's a radio program and it has nothing but messages on it to people, usually out in the bush, who don't have phones or anything. We'll listen to it tonight."

As Buff started out the door to get back to the well, he stopped and remembered. "Say, Mom, have you ever noticed the sound of an engine running in the distance? Did you see anyone working up on the road?"

"No, there was no activity along the road at all. Of course, in the jeep, I wouldn't have heard anything unless a keg of dynamite exploded right under me."

"We've been hearing it all day, off and on, and it sounds like it's coming from the far end of the lake. Are there any geophysical cats, or road-building machines or anything working up there?"

"No, not that I know of. I'm afraid there just isn't any kind of summer work scheduled for this part of the country. No jobs for anyone. I can't imagine what you heard. Maybe it's coming from the other direction and bouncing off the hill – an echo. And you know how sounds travel out here. Gracious, sometimes we can hear one another talking from half a mile or more."

"I know, but there has to be someone there talking, and I can't figure out where or what or who this is. Something else, Mom. Todd found a fish float down at the end of the lake last night."

"A fish float? How on earth would a fish float get up there?"

"That's what I'd like to know. I guess as soon as we get some time, we'll take a look down there."

But his mother had no way of knowing that a mere fish float could bring danger to the boys. How could anyone guess that? She was already jumping into chores, making preparations in case she had to leave at once. "Yes, dear," she said absently. "That would be nice."

The boys went out and began laying the pipe, but Buff was still frowning. "There's something strange about it all," he muttered almost to himself. They got the pipes connected by the time Aunt Sally called them to supper. "Well, let's leave it and eat. Then we'll give it a trial run. Okay, Todd?"

"If you say so. I'm sure anxious to see if it really works."

CHAPTER FOUR

Alone

It was almost eight o'clock when they carried their supper plates to the front screened-in porch to eat. The late sun was pouring in at a nice slanting angle so that it hit them squarely and warmly, gold and red. Alaskans loved and appreciated sunshine. Todd tore apart a piece of bread and put it out in the front yard, hoping to entice the camp robbers he heard up in the trees. Two muskrats paddled in front of the dock. Aunt Sally brought out the battery radio and turned it on.

The announcer was saying, ". . . and now for some of our messages. We have a note here from Alex Ivanovitch to Mary down at Moose Bend and he says to meet him tomorrow night at the lake in the skiff about eight o'clock, he's coming home. . . . Helen Draker called us this afternoon from downtown and said to tell Wally at Bear Bay that she arrived okay, and the doctor says the baby should be here any time. . . . A note to Packrat Pete on the Kenai says, 'I can't get the cat parts in Anchorage, they have to be shipped in from Seattle. It will make me at least three days late getting back.' It's signed by Kassilovan. . . . Here's a message to Sal, Buff, and Todd down at Loon Lake and it says, 'Job all set. I'll be at the Klondike Hotel. Must be at work by Monday. Buff and Todd, I'm really counting on you fellows this summer.' And this one is signed, 'Dad'. . . ."

Aunt Sally shut off the radio excitedly. Todd said, "Well, how about that? Gee, quite a shock to hear your name on the radio like that. Do they do that all the time?"

"Every week night. I know some people that never miss the program. Even if they don't have a message, a neighbor might."

Buff grinned. "Besides all that, how else are we going to know what our neighbors are doing?"

Aunt Sally said, "Buff!"

Todd was still reflecting. "A lot of those names sounded strange. What were they?"

"Oh, some of them were Russian. The Russians were in the area long before we were and a lot of their names are still in use. In fact, few of the native people of this area ever use an Indian or Aleut name. It's nearly all of Russian origin now and I suppose it has been for years and years."

"Are there any old Russian buildings or anything left?"

"Oh my, yes. We'll spend some time going around in town one of these days. There are Indian sites about too, even here in the woods. The Indians had a real going civilization here long before the Russians found it." Aunt

Sally jumped up. "Get Buff to tell you all he knows later on. I'd like to get ready and leave early in the morning. If Dad has to be at work Monday, we'll have to step on it. That jeep is running now on wire and prayers."

The boys started to eat their supper faster. "Okay, Aunt Sally. I'll get Buff to tell me all he knows sometime. It shouldn't take long."

Buff yelped at him.

Todd sobered and leaned confidentially toward Buff. "Will this job mean you can get the clearing done and keep the homestead?"

Buff looked at him gravely and held up his hand, then crossed two fingers, silently.

They did the dishes that night for Aunt Sally. "Now, let's give the pump the acid test. Let's go get our water supply. After all that digging and testing and pump priming, let's see if it wants to work."

Todd dashed out and pumped the handle up and down. Beautifully, reassuringly, water gushed forth. "Look at that! We did it! She's a dandy, she's a dandy!"

Buff looked satisfied. "Not bad. Not bad. The more we pump, the clearer the water will get." He grinned at Todd, hopping first on one foot, then the other, all the while working the pump handle furiously. "So have fun."

"What do you know about that? You just pump it up and down and water runs out. I never would have thought it. You know, when I get home and turn that water faucet on, I'll never take it for granted again." He looked at his sore hands that were beginning to show calluses.

"Okay, let's call it a day. Are you in the mood for a swim,

or shall we be ordinary and wash? Mom's gonna want to get up early."

They settled on washing and, while they were about it, Aunt Sally kept up a string of directions. "If the Jacksons come, you know what to do. Stay with them in the field, do any work that will hurry it along. Tell them I'll pay them when I come back. Just as soon as they leave, scatter that seed. Divide it up so you can be sure to cover the field. Oh yes, I've got as many loaves of bread as I thought would stay fresh. Keep them out on the porch where it's cooler, but still you'll probably run out. You'll have to make biscuits or pancakes or something. I'll bring some with me, though, when I come back. . . . Oh, that reminds me. Now, I may have car trouble or something so don't get too worried about me if I'm a bit late. But listen to Mukluk every night. I'll try to send at least one message to you before we leave to give you an idea how it is all coming along. Do you really think you'll be all right?"

"Mom, of course we'll be all right. We'll do the work. We'll listen for your message. You and Dad try to enjoy the trip if you can. Be careful when you're driving home by yourself. Just take it easy. There's no hurry. Better to take an extra day than push the jeep too hard and have trouble. We'll be just fine. Todd, here, is a regular baker."

Todd looked up, astonished. "Me? A baker?" All he had ever baked was a TV dinner, but he rose to the challenge, anything to help. "I guess I'm a well digger and, by tomorrow, I'll probably be a baker. Crazy country. Don't worry, Aunt Sally. Where do I find the recipes?"

"There. You see, Mom? Nothing to worry about."

"You're right. Say! Todd! I just thought of something. Unless you boys can walk and hitch a ride into town, you won't have any mail in or out. Why don't you write your folks right now and I'll mail it tomorrow. I know you sent a card that you arrived safely. But write them now and explain what is happening and why they won't be hearing from you for a while."

At first, Todd thought of trying to tell all he had seen and done – the lake, the trees, the woods, the canoe trips, the work. But he didn't. He wrote hurriedly of the main activities. He considered the letter for awhile and decided it was the most satisfactory one he had ever been able to write. He turned the phrase over and over in his mind. ". . . We will see to the cultivating and the planting." Yes, it was a good letter. It would make unusual reading in the apartment.

It seemed their heads had just touched the pillows when Aunt Sally was calling them. "Boys," she said, "I just wanted to tell you good-bye. You don't have to get up. I think everything's under control."

Buff was struggling out of bed, so Todd felt obliged to do the same. "Don't be silly, Mom, we'll help you get off."

"I'm all ready to go. I left my breakfast dishes for you. Wasn't that nice of me?"

"Of course you should leave them. Now, please, Mom, have a nice trip and take it easy – and don't worry. There's two of us and we're okay."

Aunt Sally looked at the two boys proudly. "You just bet you're okay." She added lightly, "A little sleepy, though."

They helped her carry the last of her bags and the supplies Buff's father had needed. She climbed into the jeep, started off, and waved a gay good-bye. The roar was soon lost behind the hill. They were all alone. It was suddenly a bit desolate in the woods.

CHAPTER FIVE

Bears

The boys stood a moment and looked at each other in the early, rather cloudy morning. "Well, here we are."

Todd kicked at a small stone. "Yep. Here we are." He shivered in his light T-shirt. "I don't know about you, but I'm freezing to death."

They dashed into the warm house and began fixing some breakfast. "How about it? Do you want to get back to sleep?"

"Not especially. I'm awake now."

"Let's go up and work in the field awhile. It looks like it might rain pretty soon anyway."

They ate, then divided the household chores. Todd was

still struggling with the dishes when Buff had finished making the bunks, sweeping the house, putting away clothes and scattered articles, filling the woodbox, and filling the water bucket. Todd sounded a bit discouraged.

"I just can't seem to get any speed in all this arranging and rearranging of the dishes: stacking the dirty ones, a dishpan for washing, a pan for rinsing, stacking the clean ones. I washed those cups three different times and my water is always too hot or too cold. The rinse water has more soap in it than the wash water. How did that happen? Anyway, I'll be through in a minute. Boy, I'll never take a dishwasher for granted again. How do you ever get used to it?"

Buff had been standing, grinning, listening to him. "Practice," he said. He ducked the dishcloth Todd threw.

They had no sooner gotten to the field than Buff paused. "Todd! Listen! There's that noise again. Hear it?"

"Sure I hear it." The sound was unmistakable. "You must be getting new neighbors."

"But I tell you there isn't any land open for homesteading there right now." He looked up decisively at Todd. "Let's go down there this afternoon or evening and have a look."

Light rain began to fall, so the boys headed for the house. They fixed some lunch and, sleepily, watched a loon, forlorn and wet-looking, swimming about in the lake. They both decided it would be foolish to waste dishwater and soap on that little bit of dishes, so they left them until supper. They took a short nap, and, when they awoke, it was still raining. Buff turned on the radio and got mostly static. For the first time, Todd realized dimly that it might be possible to be bored out here if you were stranded inside the cabin for long. There was no electricity: no television, no refrigerator filled with snacks, no record player, no phone, no mail coming or going, there was very little to *do.*

Although it was a bit dark in the house for reading, Todd pulled down a book on animal and bird identification, and he and Buff picked out the birds they had seen about the lake. Buff reached over and turned the radio off. "Hope it clears up before Mukluk tonight."

"At that, your radio isn't as bad as our electric one when it storms with lightning and thunder."

"I've heard that. We don't have bad static up here, except the northern lights play hob with things sometimes. But we don't have lightning and thunder. The folks have told me a couple of times that the sound we just heard was thunder but, by the time I stopped to listen, it was gone. I've never seen lightning."

"Is that right? I wonder why?"

"I don't know. I suppose we've had it sometime, but it sure isn't very common anyway."

Buff got up and walked to the porch. "You know, it isn't raining much now, but it's too wet to go back and work in the field. Let's take the canoe, go down to the end of the lake and walk back in a bit and see if we can find out something about that sound we've been hearing."

Todd looked up. "Raining too hard to work but not too hard for a boat ride? Would Aunt Sally and Uncle David approve?"

"Well, they're used to my logic. The whole field would be messy by now and I'd get mud all over my clothes, and I can't really work very well in my rain gear. I can't burn brush today. In the canoe, we won't get too wet. I've got rain clothes that cover all of me – even walking in the woods won't be too bad. You can borrow Dad's rain clothes. His hunting gear is still in the closet. I don't think of it as goofing off. I think of it as taking our pleasure when it's a bit disagreeable rather than wasting good time that could be used in the field."

Todd looked at him admiringly. "You've got a great future ahead of you. You've convinced me. Let's get the gear on."

The canoe glided silently out from the dock, through the rain-speckled lake. The boys were covered from head to toe in rain gear. Their paddles swished through the water. Todd looked about. "Every day, every kind of weather, the lake is always different and always interesting."

Buff nodded in agreement and silently lifted his canoe paddle and pointed. Todd followed the line. "Beaver." Todd fairly hugged himself with delight upon seeing the beaver. It was so much larger than the muskrats.

They continued more or less silently to the far end of the lake, back through the pads of lilies that seemed to border each bank, down to the little pond made by the beavers that the creek ran out of. They pulled up the canoe and got out. The weeds were soaking wet, but the rain had about stopped. "It seems to me," Buff said, frowning in concentration, "that the sound came from down in this direction. I thought maybe we'd follow the creek back. It should be pretty easy walking. Now, the only thing is to keep your eyes peeled. There are some brown bears here – not many, but one is plenty to bump into. The black ones should be no trouble, but those brown ones get a bit big."

Todd considered a minute. "Do you think it's safe? I hate to be a pantywaist, but –"

Buff finished for him, "But you want to keep your head? Well, so do I. Don't worry. I'm not trying to get you into a scary situation just so I can look big and you look like a city slicker. Alaskans know better than that, and those bears are too big for games. No, it isn't a hundred per cent safe, but neither is anything – even crossing the street in cities like the one you come from. At least that's what I read in the papers. But we'll keep our eyes open and we'll listen. Bears usually make lots of noise crashing around, and we'll not dash into any thick alder growth or anywhere that we can't clearly see. That's the main thing: not to take them by surprise. You can whistle and bang around if you want to warn them. Chances are if we see one at a distance, we can just turn around and leave. They can't see very well, and unless they smell us they won't even know we're around. There are lots of arguments, but most people don't think bears really look for a scrap and chase you down or anything like that."

"But not everyone agrees?"

"No, not everyone agrees. There's a man or two with a mangled leg and part of a shoulder gone that won't agree with that. You can take your choice of what to believe about brownies until you come across one, and then you'll know for sure how that one bear acted that one time."

"Oh, that's just great."

"One source of comfort though. Brown bears aren't supposed to climb trees. Just get up a tall one if you see a brownie."

Todd looked about. There were mostly spruce trees, absolutely unclimbable from his point of view. Desperately, he looked for a birch or cottonwood. "How high would it have to be?"

"Pretty high. I remember one story about a brown bear looking in an upstairs window."

Todd swallowed. "An upstairs window? Holy cow! Are you kidding me?"

"Nope. Dad and I were walking in the woods once and saw some big scratches way up in a tree that a bear had just made – real fresh scratches. Dad measured, and with his arm held as high as he could reach and with the gun length on top of that, he could just touch the end of the barrel to the scratches. These are big bears. They're the same as the Kodiak bears only they are here instead of on Kodiak. We just call them brown bears. Well, shall we go?"

"Buff, don't you think – that is, if we go, shouldn't we carry a gun or something?"

"Dad says no. He says a gun would probably get me in more trouble. He says the best thing is just to be alert and, if you see any signs, just get out of there. Say, Todd, if you're really worried, you don't have to come. Would you like to stay with the canoe? I'm just going to walk a little ways."

"No, no, I'm going." Todd looked about. He didn't feel much safer alone in the canoe. What if a bear came down to the lake? Would he know what to do? They could swim, couldn't they? Could he get the canoe out and get away fast enough? No, he was staying with Buff.

They started off, and Buff did some mental figuring out loud about the machinery noises he had heard, and the distance and all; but Todd spent his time and energy on the lookout for bears. Around every corner, against every clump of brush or trees, he expected a huge, savage, hungry bear to leap at them. A second-story window! He also kept a close lookout for trees to climb, trees that were high and that had limbs so he could get up in them. As soon as a good one came into sight, he'd heave a sigh of relief and think, I could make it now. But they would walk past it, and he'd look back regretfully, wondering how long it would take him to get back to it if they saw a bear right now, or up that hill, or in the little hollow in the side of the bank, or around that corner. How fast could bears run? Oh, he thought, why didn't I study more about such things when I had the chance? In that cavernous library at home, there must have been a book somewhere on how to deal with brown bears.

He was concentrating so hard, he almost bumped into Buff, who was suddenly standing still with his hand up for quiet. "What was that?" he whispered. "I heard something."

Todd's heart began pounding. Suddenly there was a tremendous thrashing in the brush ahead. "It's a brownie!" Todd yelled. He turned blindly and started to run.

Buff had hesitated for a minute and continued looking, but the crashing and thrashing started again and he turned and ran also. He caught up with Todd. "Let's get out of here." As they sped away, a hideous roar that sent chills clear down through their boots went ricocheting through the woods. By now, the forest seemed alive with noise. Todd stumbled and fell into the stream. Buff heard the splash and turned and helped him to his feet. "Are you okay?"

"Yes, I think so. Let's get going." Buff put an arm about Todd. "Are you hurt?"

Todd shook his head, dazed for a moment. "No, I'm okay." He started to run again. The crashing seemed to be farther behind them, but the hideous noise sounded as if in pursuit of them. They didn't take time to look around.

They ran until Todd suddenly saw the most welcome sight in his life: the canoe peacefully swaying on the lake.

Buff was out of breath but said, haltingly, "Now – whatever you do – take it easy getting in. This is no time to hurry. It's better to take another minute than capsize the canoe."

Shaking with fear and fatigue, Todd forced himself to grasp the sides of the boat slowly and steadily and lower himself in. Buff followed and pulled the rope off a stump he had anchored it to. Not until they were well out into the lake did they pause to look around. "Are we far enough out to stop?" Todd asked fearfully.

"I think so. If a bear did try to follow us, we could certainly get away from him with our head start."

But they could see nothing. There was no noise: no crashing through the brush, no roars. Todd still didn't feel too secure about it. What, he thought, just what if a bear *would* follow us home? Would we be safe there? If they could look into a second-story window, they must be awfully big and awfully strong. Even the cabin now seemed vulnerable to him.

Buff was asking, "How are you? You sure got your face banged up."

Todd absently felt his face, then said, "Ouch!" involuntarily. "I didn't even realize it was hurt, really. What a crazy thing to do – slip and fall into a creek when a brownie is chasing you. I'm sorry, Buff."

"Don't be silly. You couldn't help it and we're okay. At least I am. We'll get home and fix you up." The rain had started again and they huddled, wet and dripping in the canoe. They paddled in silence, looking back every now and then to see if anything was visible or following them.

The cabin, which earlier had seemed barren to Todd and made him restless when he was housebound, now looked like a haven. Inside was warmth, food, rest, comfort, and security—he hoped—from bears that looked in upstairs windows. It was good to get home! They shed wet clothes. Buff poked up the fire and added fuel, then carried in more wood so it could be drying out. Todd inspected his scratches and bruises.

"I don't think it's going to amount to much. It just hurt for a minute there."

"That's good. Well, let's hang up these clothes to dry and get the chores done. I guess I can measure out that seed like Mom told me. There's not much hurry. The Jacksons can't cultivate while it's wet. But it's one job I can do inside. Then we'll have to think about getting supper. It takes me a long time to do that. How are you at cooking?"

"Who, me? Oh, when I have to get my own dinner, I just

go to the refrigerator and make a sandwich and eat up the leftovers and maybe have some milk or some pop. Sometimes I just run down to the restaurant next door."

Buff nodded. "Just as I thought. We'd better plan on spending a lot of time getting supper. If you feel like it, you can help me parcel out this seed."

"Sure, I'm fine. I parcel out seed the very best when my face is a bloody mess."

Buff grinned. "As I said before, you're crazy."

They went onto the back porch and opened up a dusty gunny sack filled with seed. "What kind of seed is this?"

"Brome grass. We're just going to spread it. We don't expect to raise too much. It takes about two or three years after clearing and working the ground to get a decent crop. By that time, we hope to be ready to go into business: grain for livestock, or potatoes, something useful. This grass is just to prove up the homestead and get the soil in shape."

"Tell me once more why we're putting it in smaller sacks. Don't get me wrong: I'm crazy about the job, but I just want to know why."

"Well, we can only afford this much seed. It has to plant the whole field. If we didn't ration it out, I'd probably put most of it on one little corner and not have any left for the rest of the field. Then, too, if we spread it, we can only carry so much. You can take a bag and I'll take one." They opened the rest of the gunny sacks and finished the job.

Then they began rattling around in the kitchen. "How do you cook without a refrigerator? Where *is* everything?"

"Well, we have to get some cold water and mix the powdered milk in it. We open cans for what we want to eat.

In the winter, we have our frozen meat and all in an outdoor refrigerator. At least that's what we call it. It's just that little shed out there. Trappers and people who are gone a lot and even some homesteaders build a little place called a "cache" up in a tree to store their food – or some place where the animals can't get to it too easily. But in the summer, it's cans. If we want potatoes or beans or rice, we cook them. There isn't much of anything just to grab up and eat."

Todd assumed a dramatic pose. "I'll never take Aunt Sally for granted again." He suddenly grimaced. "That cricked my neck. I must have broken that too when I fell. How stupid of me to have overlooked a broken neck."

Buff grinned. "I don't know what we ever did around here for laughs before you came, except listen to the loons, of course." He looked appraisingly at Todd. "You're the most banged-up cook I ever looked at. Have you seen your face? Maybe you'd better take an aspirin."

"I'm okay. Come on, tell me what to cook. I'm starved to death. I've been chased by a bear, we ate breakfast at something like midnight, it seemed, and just a sandwich for dinner. Ugh! That reminds me – we left the dishes, didn't we?"

"Yes, we did, and that's one thing about dishes: they wait for you. Well, do you want potatoes or rice? We don't have time to cook beans. I think you have to soak them. We can open some canned moose, or canned salmon."

"Rice! That's what we'll have. You have to peel potatoes, don't you? We'll have rice. That sounds simple. Yes, let's have some salmon. I haven't had any yet. Salmon and rice sounds good. You get the other stuff out and I'll cook the rice. Okay?"

"Okay." Buff went out to pump some cold water for the powdered milk. He set the table, opened the canned salmon, got the bread and butter from the coolness of the back porch where they were kept, and cleaned some raw carrots.

When he came in, he stared in disbelief at the two huge pans full of rice on the stove.

"What in the world?"

"Buff, have you ever cooked rice?"

"Well, yes, but not that much. Don't you know it swells up when it cooks?"

"I'm beginning to suspect so," Todd spoke lightly, but he looked stricken.

"Don't worry, Todd," Buff said kindly. "We have to have something to feed the camp robbers."

CHAPTER SIX

Bad News

They ate supper, and Buff goodnaturedly refused to notice that Todd was trying to eat up all the rice. "Don't you want to try some of this salmon? It's king. That's the very best. Probably can't even buy real king where you come from."

"Well, I'll just taste it. I'll use up my space with this rice. It sure is good, isn't it?"

"Terrific. Look, Todd, you're going to make yourself sick. You don't have to eat all that rice. We'll give it to the birds."

"I'm just trying to get strong. If I'm going to get chased by bears every day or so –"

"Todd, you know what? I've been thinking. I don't think we were chased by a bear today."

Todd's forkful of rice clattered to the plate. "You don't think we were chased by a bear? Look at my face. Remember how I fell down? Listen, I wasn't the only one running.

You just about passed me several times. What about that awful noise?" He shuddered, remembering.

"I don't know about that awful noise, but I'd sure like to know. Let's go back tomorrow if we get a chance. I'll bet you anything that wasn't a bear."

"Well, what are you going to do? How can you prove it? Go back and, if we get run out again, say you were wrong?"

"No, but we can go back and look for tracks or for brush beat down, or something. The way that thing was carrying on, there should be *something* to show for it all."

"If it wasn't a bear, what could it have been? A moose? Do they make noise like that?"

"No, they don't; and a bear doesn't make noise quite like that either. Todd, there's something funny going on down there. I'm just sure of it."

"Real funny. Some joke. Scare people to death."

"I guess I didn't mean *funny*. I meant strange. Well, we'll see. Let's get these dishes going. We don't want to miss Mukluk tonight."

Buff was fixing the fire and starting some popcorn when their message arrived. "Hey, Todd, did you hear that?" he called to the kitchen where Todd was. "Message to us from Mom saying she and Dad were leaving Anchorage at two o'clock."

Todd put away some dishes. "Good."

Buff had just started to turn the radio down when the announcer said, "Wait! We have another emergency message, just in. This is to Todd and Buff at Loon Lake also – from Dr. Pendleton. It says, 'Your mother and father both injured in wreck about four this afternoon. They are all right, repeat, they are all right, but hospitalized in Anchorage. Your father has a broken leg, your mother will probably be released in a day or so." The announcer then repeated his emergency message.

Todd turned, dish still in hand and looked at Buff's face. "Buff! Oh, Buff! I'm so sorry. What will we do?"

Buff turned. "We don't *do* anything, I guess. Nothing we can do." Despairingly, he put down the corn popper. "Well, with a broken leg, there goes Dad's job, there goes the summer money, there goes the homestead." He buried his head in his hands for a minute.

"Oh, *gosh,*" Todd said sympathetically. He almost felt like crying. "Oh, Buff, I guess things just couldn't be worse for you, could they?"

Buff looked up slowly. "You just don't know. Yes, they sure could. The folks are alive at least. A broken leg is something you get over. Whatever is wrong with Mom must not be too serious if she's getting out in a day or so. The cabin hasn't burned down, and the bear didn't catch us. Sure, things could be worse." He sighed and put the popper back on the top of the stove. "But I guess things could always be worse and I don't know that it makes a broken leg easier to bear by saying you're glad both legs weren't broken. If only I could get hold of some money! If only I could work, but there just isn't anything around here. The canneries won't hire anyone my age. Money, money!"

The boys discussed every angle, trying to find a way out. "Well," Buff finally said. "The best way we can help, I guess, is just to go ahead. They'll send messages if they want us to do differently. We've got the seed. We'll get it planted.

If someone buys our improvements, the planting will make the place worth more."

While they were eating their popcorn, the Jacksons drove in to tell them about the Mukluk message, to make sure they had heard it. "Yes, thanks, Mr. Jackson. I heard what there was. I suppose we'll get more word later."

Mrs. Jackson brought the boys a big can of moose stew and a box of hot rolls and biscuits. "I didn't know how you boys were doing in the cooking line."

"We're doing fine, Mrs. Jackson, but that surely looks good. Thanks a lot."

Mr. Jackson went on to tell Buff that he wouldn't be able to get in to do the cultivating for at least a week now; the rain was holding him up and he had just broken a part and so must make a trip to Anchorage. Would the boys like to go?

Buff hesitated, then said, "I guess not, Mr. Jackson, but thanks. Mom gave us jobs to do. I guess we had better stay here and get them done."

Mrs. Jackson fussed over them a bit and wondered anxiously if they were *sure* they would be all right with no folks and no close neighbors.

When they were gone, Buff explained, "Maybe we should have gone, but it's a long trip and they just have a little jeep, and we wouldn't have any place to stay in Anchorage when we got there and"—his voice faltered—"and, well, I told you about the work. It's important right now for me to get the most work done that I can."

It had been a long, long day; full of physical action and fear, warm food, and, finally, worry. The boys sat for a long

time in front of the wood stove with its front door open so they could watch the flames. They talked, almost hypnotically. Todd tried to explain how it was with his father and Jamey. Buff talked of the constant worry of money and how important it was to his father and to all of them that they prove themselves on the homestead.

Todd burst out suddenly, "Buff, I don't know much about your father, I guess. But I know my dad has money. I wonder why your father doesn't just borrow some? After all, Dad's his brother, even if they never seem to see much of each other."

"I don't know. I just know Dad won't consider borrowing the money like that. Maybe my father is like yours, Todd, only in a different way. He thinks he's the adventurer in the family; in a way, maybe even a failure. He wants to make a go of the homestead on his own. He told me that he had to make it up to Mom for all the moving around. You know, probably she'd rather have had a big house and all instead of bumming around and roughing it. Your dad was always proving things in sports, and mine needs to prove himself on the homestead. I've thought about it and thought about it. Maybe all fathers are like this, or maybe it's just our family." He paused, then said thoughtfully, "What do you suppose we'll be like when we're fathers? What will our sons say about us?"

"I won't be like my father or Jamey. I *can't* be. I think I'll be more understanding and not always telling about my touchdowns and track meets."

"But what if your son is like your father or Jamey. Will you understand him?"

"I see your point. Funny old world, isn't it? I always thought being a grownup and getting away would fix everything, but maybe it's more complicated than I thought. . . . You know? I think I'd like to go into something where I could be independent. I can't work as well with people as Dad or Jamey can. They're so friendly and bright and, oh, I don't know, so out-and-out."

Buff turned and looked at Todd's troubled face as the little lights from the flames danced about it. "You know something? I think you do a lot better than you think you do. I don't know Jamey but he couldn't have fit in any better here than you do. Not everyone in the world goes for that type. You just think they do. The world is just full of people who never played halfback in their lives – you're not the only one."

Todd looked thoughtfully at Buff. "Gee, when you put it that way –"

The talk continued until the fire was almost gone and the boys almost too sleepy to get up and go to bed. Todd made one last remark: "Just remember, Buff. I can give sermons too. The world is full of people who have thought of ways of making money too."

Buff chuckled. "Maybe you're right at that. Tomorrow is another day." But his last thought was of his mother and dad. He wondered if they hurt very much right now.

CHAPTER SEVEN

Two-Legged Bears

The boys slept hard and late. The rain fell in rhythmic patterns on the roof over their bunks. There was no bright sun to wake them. Loons cried mournfully in the wet morning and, across the gray mist that hung over the lake, the grebes awakened and squawked back. It was chilly in the house when Buff woke. He started a fire in the wood stove and put some water on the propane stove to make some cups of instant hot chocolate. When Todd stirred, he carried one to him.

"Hi. How are you this morning?"

Todd shook his head and accepted the cup. "Wow! I don't know when I've slept like that. I feel drugged. Boy, you really hear that rain on the roof, don't you? I like it." He sat up and sipped the hot chocolate. "Pretty good service around here. Keep this up and I may come back next summer."

"How are your bruises and all? Are you ready for another trip?"

Todd gingerly felt his face and winced a couple of times. "Feels like I've got a broken nose, but since I don't walk on it I guess it won't keep me from a trip. Where are we going?"

"I want to go check the end of the lake today. We'll take some sandwiches and the binoculars and we'll stay awhile if we have to."

"You mean if we *can*. Yesterday I had the feeling we stayed plenty long."

Todd got out of bed and walked to the front room and sat down. "Buff, you really don't think it was a bear, do you?"

"I sure don't and I want to find out what it is. This is a perfect chance. The well is dug, we can't work in the field, and when Dad and Mom come home they might need a lot of waiting on. I want to find out while we can. Now, you don't have to go if you don't want to." He glanced quickly at Todd.

"Sure I'm going. Who else is going to yell 'brownie' at you and get you to run? Besides, there's nothing to do here but cook rice and I've already done that."

Buff laughed, but he was secretly relieved. He hadn't realized how much he wanted Todd to go along. That roar yesterday was loud.

They fixed and ate breakfast, thought of all the reasons why they should leave the dishes, and convinced themselves. Buff compromised by putting them in a dishpan of hot water to soak. Then they fixed some sandwiches and a thermos of hot bouillon; made up the bunk beds and cleaned the house a bit. Todd carried out some leftovers and tried to find a dry sheltered place for them where the camp robbers would find them. When he came back, he said, "Buff. Just once more. If that wasn't a bear and it wasn't a moose and it wasn't anything else, what on earth was it? Do you mean we're going nuts? What's the Alaskan term you hear about– cabin fever?"

"Todd, I don't know. I've tried to think of everything it could possibly be, even to freak noises and jets crashing the sound barrier at exactly the wrong time and echoes bouncing around. We do have jets that fly over now and then." He hesitated as if he might say something, then changed his mind, and said instead, "First, maybe I'm wrong. Let's see if we can find any tracks or anything that looks like a bear. A new bear story comes out every year. We might as well add ours to the lot."

They loaded gear and thoughtfully took their places in the boat and paddled quietly down the lake. Todd already knew without being told that they must be quiet in the canoe if they wanted to observe beavers, muskrats, and birds. But Buff turned to Todd, saying emphatically, "Let's be extra, extra quiet. Yesterday we made noise to warn the bears but today, let's not. We'll be real careful and, if we find tracks or any sign, we won't go any farther. Okay?"

"Whatever you say." But he remembered yesterday's advice on safety from bears: don't surprise them.

They got out. Buff picked up the binoculars, but indicated they could leave the lunch, covered up in the bottom of the canoe. "Now," he whispered to Todd, "be on the lookout for tracks. They would be real, real big, probably big enough to put a ten-gallon hat in. They might not be too plain since the rain, but we should still be able to see at least a few after the way he was charging around. Oh yes, there might be bits of fur caught in the brush. Or there might be droppings."

Slowly and silently, the boys started off. Todd tried to behave like a detective and look for the signs, but he was still thinking of that awful roar yesterday and of bears that could reach into second-story windows. He started looking for trees again. How far was the canoe now? He looked back.

They continued walking, then Buff stopped. "Here is where we were yesterday. Now, we never did see the bear but we heard him up ahead here. Let's go on just a little. Okay?"

Todd nodded in agreement, standing behind Buff and peering ahead as far as he could see. They walked another few yards. Buff turned. "I'll tell you that was no bear yesterday. There's not a thing here."

But just as he said it, faint sounds came to his ears. Todd turned on his heel, ready for flight. His heart pounded, and his blood felt as cold as Loon Lake when he went swimming. Buff put a restraining hand on him. "Listen a minute," he whispered.

There was a medley of low sounds – like pounding or working of some kind. Then they caught the sounds of voices, garbled, but voices undeniably.

Buff looked at Todd. "No bear. Let's get out of this creek

area. Let's climb that hill and keep under cover. Maybe we'll just find out what's going on."

Buff led the way and quickly they left the creek and climbed a green hill, being as careful as they could about noise. "Oh boy," Todd whispered as the twigs and branches snapped under him, "some Indian I'd make."

As they rounded the top of the hill, they saw a couple of great, huge rocks rearing up from the ground, moss-covered with grass growing on them, left from some glacial period, as a baby might throw blocks on a living-room rug and go away and leave them.

"Look at that!" exclaimed Todd. "Those are about the biggest rocks I ever saw. What do you suppose they weigh?" He looked from one to the other.

"Many tons. They look kind of funny out here by themselves, don't they? Well, let's use them. We could get lots closer just by keeping in the brush, but these boulders are handier." He kept in line with one of the rocks and came up behind it. Todd was close at his heels. As they peered around, they could see movement in the valley below, near the creek, which was around the bend of the hill from where they had been on the stream.

"What are they doing?"

"I don't know. Here, let me get the binoculars out." He sat down in the wet weeds on the hill and looked through the glasses. He wiped little peppery raindrops from them from time to time. Then he handed the glasses to Todd. "See what you can make of it. I can't see too well. Leaves and trees in the way, but they're working at something."

Todd took a turn. "Do you mean it was people that scared us out yesterday, Buff?"

"It just begins to look that way. Maybe they thought it was a joke." The more he thought about it, the more plausible that sounded. "Yes sir, I'll bet they scared us for fun and probably had a big laugh." He looked at Todd, who had the binoculars, peering from beneath his rain hat. "Can you see anything?"

"Just like you said. They all seem to be working. I can't see what they're doing. I see two fellows right now. How many did you see?"

"I thought I saw three." He picked up the glasses. "Todd! Look through the leaves on that big cottonwood, on the right-hand side of it. I can see a truck or tractor or something."

"You're right! That must have been the noise we heard."

"But how did it ever get there? From here, the closest road is a long, long way. They must have had to build a road, either from the main highway or down the beach. But why? They're not just on a camping trip – not spending that kind of money and effort to build a whole road."

"Gee, Buff, I just don't know. As I said, even Sherlock Holmes would be stuck here. Hey! Maybe they're government crews of some kind. Maybe they're doing some work out here – you know, like in the movies and stories where government people are always doing things way back in the boondocks. Forest service or something."

"Well, it's possible, but nobody has said anything about it. Up here, something like that is known to everyone right away. Well, there's one way to tell: let's just go ask them. If they're government workers, they won't mind even if they do believe in scaring kids. If they are new neighbors or something, it's the only friendly thing to do." He rose, a bit stiffly, from the wet weeds and peered around the rock. "Let me look at that truck again. If it's a government truck, it will probably have something on it – Department of Interior, or Fish and Wildlife, something like that." He looked but could not see well enough. "I don't know," he said dubiously. "I can't get in a good line of vision with it, but it sure doesn't look like a government vehicle."

"Maybe they're drilling for oil."

"It's possible, but word like that usually gets around pretty fast." Buff started down the hill. "Coming?"

"Well, I – I – guess so. Should we be so out in the open, though? I mean, just in case?"

Buff hesitated. "Maybe you're right. It's kind of silly, but just in case." As they circled down and a bit to the right, Buff suddenly slipped on some wet grass and weeds and fell. Just as he did, the hideous roar they had heard yesterday sounded again.

Buff looked up and grabbed at Todd's leg just as Todd was about to run. He pulled him down with him. "Wait a minute. Just wait. I know that's no bear." He swung the binoculars around and looked carefully in every direction. The noise resounded again and, as he looked, he saw the two men below pause and look up, then start walking up the creek bank.

At that minute, Todd spied something. "Oh, Buff, don't look now. There was a third man all right. He's making all that noise and he's looking right at us. He doesn't look like

he's playing a joke and he doesn't look like a friendly new neighbor."

Buff froze for a minute. "Look away from him, Todd, and pretend you haven't seen him. Then I'll look through my glasses." When Buff located the man through the binoculars, he gasped. Crouched behind a clump of weeks was a heavy-set man with a coarse black scraggly beard. He was making a hideous noise. He held a huge monkey wrench in his hand, and he was the meanest-looking man Buff had ever seen.

"Oh boy, oh boy. I don't know what the trouble is, but I don't want him to use that wrench on us. Listen, Todd, those two others are coming too. You start yelling, Brownie! Brownie! and start running."

Todd stared at him, "Brownie?" he whispered.

Buff didn't argue or explain but scrambled to his feet and started shouting, "Brownie! There's a brownie! Run for your life!" He pulled Todd with him, shouting all the way. "Bears, bears!"

He wouldn't let Todd stop until they were in the canoe. Quickly, they got in, started paddling, and headed for home. "Look around every once in a while and see if you see anyone, okay?"

When they were safely out in the middle of the lake, Todd said, "What was that all about?"

"Well, maybe we made them think we hadn't seen them. But I'm not too sure. You keep looking back now and then. Whatever they are doing, it's something they don't want anyone else to know about. That was no joke."

"I didn't laugh anyway."

They were just about to round the bend and go through the path in the lilies to the small dock, when Buff took out his binoculars and scanned the lake shore, all up and down. What he saw shook him clear down to his waterproof boots. "Todd, one of those men is following us along the shore."

Todd felt his heart lurch. "He is? Holy smoke, what do we do now?"

"I don't know. What's even more important, I don't know what they're going to do."

"I guess we didn't fool them, huh?"

"Maybe they just want to make sure."

Todd tried a bit of levity. "Oh, well, I always knew acting wasn't one of my strong points. You even had to yell 'brownie' for me – one word and I couldn't say my lines." He looked at Buff, "No time for jokes?"

"Oh, I don't know. Maybe times like these are the test of a real sense of humor." He put down the glasses. "He's still skulking around – following us and dodging behind trees. Maybe he's just trying to see if they really did fool us. In that case, playing dumb and innocent is the best bet." Just as they rounded the bend, he took another last look. "I want to place where he is as best I can, and as soon as we land I'm going to scoot out in the woods and try to see what he is doing and how close he's coming."

Todd didn't know his hands were shaking until he tried to unload the canoe. Buff said, "I'm going up on that hill to watch. I probably won't be able to see him unless he comes along the edge of the swamp or the clearing. Come on up when you've unloaded."

Todd nodded. He carried the supplies into the cabin, stoked up the fire and threw another log on. Then he stepped outside and looked for Buff up on the hill. There was an eerie quality to the late gray, dull morning. Todd felt the hairs on the back of his neck rising. Was there really someone after them? Where was safety? He tried to calm his feelings and he forced himself away from the cabin and concentrated on the hill where Buff was.

"See anything?"

"No, I don't. Maybe we were just imagining things. Maybe he was still trying to scare us for fun. I don't suppose he's really pursuing us. Why would he? Maybe he's just walking up the lake to see where we go, see where our house is."

Todd finished by nodding his head, "The better to kill you, my dear."

"Oh, come on." He searched the woods again. "I don't know whether to feel scared or downright foolish."

"How about both?"

"Todd, the thing is, why would anyone want to hurt us?"

"I don't know, Buff, and I know I'm just a city dude and maybe I'm reading too much in this. Maybe I've seen too many westerns, but I'll tell you that I don't think that man was scaring us for fun and I think they didn't want us around. Now, maybe they wouldn't actually *do* anything to us – I don't know about that either. But I'd bet anything that whatever they were doing back there, they weren't having a Sunday school picnic."

Buff sighed. "I think you're right. I hate to be melodramatic, like a kid playing detective, but I think you're right. Whatever they are doing, they don't want us around. Next time, we've got to find out what it is they are doing."

Todd gasped. "Next time?"

"Why not? We know now it's not bears, but people. We know they're not friendly. We know we mustn't be seen and that we'll have to be very, very careful. Next time, we'll walk down through the woods and not take the canoe. They'll be looking for us to come by the lake if we come again."

"Buff, if they are really doing something wrong and if we are in any kind of danger, maybe we should go tell someone."

"I thought about it. But what would we say? That we saw some men in the woods and they tried to chase us? Who would believe us? We don't know who they are or what they're doing. It's thirty miles to town and the one patrolman covers a hundred-mile area or so. But if we could get to town and could get a patrolman, what would we tell him? He'd just say it was our imagination, or that if some men were working and didn't want us around, then to stay away. They aren't on our land, you know." Buff looked at Todd. "At least I don't want to be the one to tell them. Do you?"

"No-o-o. No, I guess you're right."

They squatted on the hill, Buff with the glasses propped in his hands, Todd looking about him slowly, constantly, in a full circle. "Funny," Buff said, "We were so sure they were dangerous back there, but when you stop to think about it and get away a little, it doesn't seem very likely."

"Maybe," Todd said, "but I still know where I am. I'm

out in the rain in the middle of the woods watching for a mean-looking man that has followed us a mile or so."

These terse words had a final sound to them: like the hollow, final sound of nails being pounded into a coffin. Todd shivered, then Buff shivered. "When you add it up like that, I think you're right." Buff turned about. "Look, let's decide this once and for all and stop spending half our energy wondering if we're being foolish. We've already been run out twice and we've already felt scared. Now, it never has to go any further than us, nobody has to know, but let's just decide right now that they are mean, maybe dangerous. If we scout around and find there's nothing to it and we've been silly, then we've been silly and it's our secret."

Todd sighed. "Good thinking. I'm with you. I agree that not knowing is the worst."

"All right. Now –" Buff was interrupted by a moving figure coming into view in his binoculars. He drew in his breath sharply. "Todd, Todd. He's still coming. It just took him a long time to walk around the swamp, I guess."

Todd grabbed the glasses and looked. "It's the same one. It's that same man. Old Blackbeard." He looked intently for a moment. "I don't think he has his monkey wrench, though."

Buff scrambled to his feet. "Let's get out of here. Let's get in the house. I want to pretend that everything is normal and fine."

They sneaked down the hill, around in front of the cabin and in the front door. They quickly shook off their rain hats and coats. Buff went over and turned the knob on the back door that locked it on the outside. "The front door doesn't have a lock on it, but I'll hook the screen door. That's the best we can do."

Todd was watching all the preparations. "You want to act normal and you go around locking all the doors?"

"I want to go on looking normal," Buff said grimly. Then he took down the high-powered rifle from the wall. "This is the only gun Dad left."

"Are you – are you going to use that thing?"

"I sure hope not. But if he starts in that door, I mean to stop him."

"Could you shoot a man, Buff"

"I don't know. I don't think I could aim to kill a person, but I think I could do enough shooting to make him nervous He checked the gun to be sure it was loaded, then made sure it was on safety. "No, I want you to fix us some lunch and set it up on a table out on the porch. We'll take the kitchen table out, or put two chairs together or something. Then we'll take the radio out."

"Eat on the porch on a rainy old day like this? I'm still cold and wet."

"Yes, but I want this fellow to think we saw nothing that would bother them. We'll eat, play cards, listen to the radio, and tell him things he wants to hear. We'll talk real loud, about getting run out by bears. You know."

"I get you. I get you. Okay, I'm going to make some hot chocolate. At least I don't have to eat cold stuff."

"Right. Tell you what: I'll set up the table. I want us to get out there as soon as we can. You fix something real fast. I'm going to sneak a look and see if I can see him. Okay?"

"Okay." Todd went to the kitchen, put some water on to heat, and, with shaking hands, tried to make sandwiches. He kept buttering his fingers instead of the bread. It was unbelievable. A man was honest-to-goodness after them. He might be peering in the window this very moment ready to throw a knife, or shoot. Hastily, Todd looked up at the window, then crossed the room, knife and bread still in hand, to look out another window. He stopped, stock still. He could have sworn he heard something. A shuffle? Someone sliding about—? Where was the gun? If the man got Buff, could he use the gun?

"It's way too quiet in here," Buff said as he came in from the back porch.

Startled, Todd dropped his knife with a clatter.

"Well, it *was* too quiet in here. We're supposed not to have a care in the world, remember?"

"Oh yes, not a care in the world, not a care in the world. Ha ha."

Buff went over to get the radio. He carried it out to the porch and turned it on. From there, he shouted, "Hey, let's eat!"

When he came back, he said, "How's dinner—? What on earth are you doing?" For Todd was standing stiff in the middle of the living room, spreading and spreading the knife over and over on the same slice of bread.

Todd looked down at his hands. "Oh, oh, yes, the rest of the sandwich is in the kitchen." He dashed out. "Hot chocolate is about ready." As Buff came out, he whispered, "Did you see anything?"

"Yes. He's right out in the side yard behind the big spruce, watching and listening. He's hiding. It will be swell, though, he's right in line to see in the side of the front porch where we'll be."

Todd tried to pour hot water into the hot chocolate cups. The pan shook against the cup like a little drum. "Oh sure, it's going to be swell."

They carried the food out and Todd tried not to look in the direction where the man was hiding. Buff was carrying on like a man on the stage.

"I guess he is on stage," Todd thought, miserably. He couldn't get his sandwich to go down. It just seemed to stick in his throat. His hand was shaking so he couldn't get the hot chocolate to his mouth without spilling. He momentarily expected to be pitched forward, splattering all the lunch, with an arrow in his back. I'll never see another western or murder picture as long as I live, he thought.

Buff was going on, "Boy, how about this for bear country? Wait 'til the folks come back and we tell them about those two brownies! Boy, did you see that first one? I saw something crashing in the brush and he was as big as a two-story building. Wait 'til the folks get home this fall! Hey, let's play cards –"

Todd was moaning to himself. Now why did Buff have to say the folks were gone? A clear invitation to get them wiped out.

Buff was kicking him under the table. "Come on," he whispered. "Talk to me. If they know the folks are gone and there's just a couple of kids who think they saw a big bear, they won't be concerned – maybe."

Todd still thought it was all wrong. In the movies, they always pretended that there was another five hundred men in the fort, never less than there actually was, or that the cavalry was on its way. Oh sure, lay our cards on the table and we'll fool him. We fooled them so much down there that he followed us a whole mile or so home through the miserable woods. He gulped a drink of chocolate that finally pushed the bite of sandwich down. "Yes," he said aloud, "after a bear chase, I always say, it's hot chocolate!" He laughed weirdly at his own joke.

Buff rose and whispered, "I'm going to go in the house and take a peek out one of the windows." Loudly, he said, "I'm going to get some more hot chocolate. Want some?"

"Yes." Todd started to rise, but Buff nudged him. "Sit still." Todd was alone on the porch. Oh boy, oh boy. I wonder, he thought, if I'm supposed to keep on making noise. Maybe I should tell jokes and laugh at them. Then he'll think we're just plain crazy and maybe *that* will fool him. He reached over and turned the radio up. Might as well die with the bands playing.

When Buff came back out, he said, "Well, I think he's leaving. I peeked from behind a curtain for a while and he was starting to move back. I don't think he suspects a thing."

Todd breathed a big sigh of relief and grabbed up another sandwich. It went down better. "Doesn't suspect a thing? Are you out of your mind? You think he's standing out there in the rain for a half an hour because he doesn't suspect a thing?"

"I mean I think he's reassured now. He doesn't believe

we're anything to worry about." He grabbed up some chocolate and sandwich and ate hurriedly. "Let's give him just a little time and then we'll follow him."

"Follow him? Why?"

"Well, we've already decided that we've got to find out what is going on down there. I'm just sure he won't be expecting us right now. We'll go slow and easy. If we're careful, we can get real close. There's lots of undergrowth near the stream. Okay?"

They gathered up the food, the tables, and the radio and took them in. Buff considered, then stashed in the lunch dishes with the breakfast dishes in the dishpan and added a bit more hot water, and let them all soak.

Todd was changing some of his wet clothes. There was a rank smell of wet, steamy wool in the house. Buff handed him a pocket knife. "Let's each take one and a bit of twine. You never know." He paused, thinking. "I want to take the glasses again, and some candy bars." He gave Todd a couple of candies. "Stick 'em in your pocket." He looked at the gun, then at Todd. "I just don't know."

They had the fire banked and were ready to go when Buff looked again at the gun and considered. "No, I'm not going to take it. We're just going to be careful and not get caught. Anyway, I'll bet they don't have a gun. It's probably more dangerous to carry one than not." He looked at Todd. "What do you think?"

"I think I'd better be ready to outrun a monkey wrench coming at me."

Buff grinned. "I don't think Dad would approve of our taking it. After all, I'm not going down there to shoot anyone or to hold up three big men. If there is going to be any excitement, one of us might end up shooting the other."

Todd opened the door. "That last convinced me."

Buff started out. "Now, let's be real, real careful and watch way ahead. He's got enough of a head start to almost be there if he doesn't stop for something, but there's always that chance – he might get a pebble in his boot or something and, if he's near us and happens to glance back – well, we don't want to be caught, do we?"

"Amen."

CHAPTER EIGHT

Captured and Lost

The rain had almost stopped, but the sky was leaden, dark, and gray; and the weeds and brush were soaking wet. The boys skirted the big swamp and headed back into the woods. They stopped every once in a while, trying to catch any sounds of a person walking, a person that would probably not be too careful. They made it to the big rocks, and once again hid behind them. Buff suddenly held up a warning hand. Their man was just ahead of them and just going into the camp. The boys slid down the hill, away from the stream bed. They could hear the camp noises. The trees and brush were very thick, exactly the kind Buff had warned about because of bears; but now, the foliage was welcome. When they were close enough to make out the words, they stopped behind some alder bushes.

Old Blackbeard was saying, "Naw, they're just a couple of kids. I watched them for a while. There's no one else around – I heard 'em say so." He stopped and laughed, a rather superior, cruel sound. "Even heard one of 'em say how big the bear was that chased him."

Buff nudged Todd and grinned. Todd held up a finger, showing their scheme had been successful. Buff whispered, "I've got to get closer. I can hear but I can't see anything."

"You'd better stay right where you are. They'll say something pretty soon. We'll find out what they're doing."

This time Buff conceded to Todd's wisdom. He stayed still behind the weeds: wet and chilly, but quiet.

One of the men was talking, "Hey, how about some grub? Watchin' those kids eat made me hungry. Where's Hank?"

"He took a load down to the site. Be back in a little bit. Here's some hot coffee. There're doughnuts in there. That do? I think there's a can of beans left."

Todd leaned over. "What does that mean?"

"I'm beginning to get an idea and it answers lots of questions. Todd! If this is what I think it is, it's serious."

"Serious? I never doubted it from the time that guy chased me with a monkey wrench. But what is it?"

Before Buff could answer, he heard one of the men say, "Okay, that gear's mended. I think I hear Hank coming. Let's fix something to eat and then we'll all go down and set it again."

The sound of the vehicle came nearer. Buff could hardly contain himself. "See, Todd? See? There *was* a vehicle that we were hearing. Do you know what they're doing?"

"No, no, no, no. Tell me. All I know is I got roared at and chased. For heaven's sake, what are they doing?"

"They must be catching salmon illegally."

"What? All this rumpus over a few fish? Why, for cryin' out loud! That's just about like getting a ticket for speeding, isn't it? Why all the excitement?"

"Oh no, no. I don't mean sports fishing. I mean they're fishing commercially. It sounds to me like they're fishing up this stream somewhere. I didn't know there was a very good place here, but maybe there's a pool. You see, the salmon come into the streams to spawn and it's against the law to catch them there. There are just certain places where you can fish and, even in the Inlet, you've got to be a mile from the mouth of the river, a certain distance away from another fisherman, things like that. Why, in a spawning stream, it would be, like–like, well–"

"Like shooting fish in a barrel?"

"Only more so."

"Even so, would it be worth all this?"

"Oh yes, if anything is worth illegal action, this is. It could mean thousands and thousands of dollars."

"Really? And what if they get caught?"

"If they get caught, they get a fine: a big one, but usually not for as much money as they might make. Maybe even a jail sentence, but it's not likely. But the worst part of it isn't that they make so much more money than others, it's that they spoil the fishing for others for years to come. If they keep all these salmon from spawning, there won't be any for the next years."

Todd was listening with interest, trying to digest all this news. "If we know all this, can we go get help now?"

"Yes. I think that's just what we should do. We'll get into town as soon as we can and get an enforcement officer from the Fish and Wildlife or Fish and Game or a patrolman—anyone we can find." Buff hesitated. "I'm sure that's what this is all about, but I wish I could see for sure where the net is." He looked at Todd. "I wonder how they get rid of the fish?"

"I give up."

Buff was craning his neck about. "It looks like they've hidden the camp in the bushes. I wonder how far down in the stream they have their nets strung? No wonder they chased us when we started up the creek the other day."

He became so interested, he got careless. Todd saw him start to slip and grabbed for him. "Buff."

Buff didn't slip far, but far enough to make noise. He scrambled to his feet. "Did they hear us? Let's get going!"

But it was too late. Commotion was rampant in the fishermen's camp. "Oh, just some boys, huh? Didn't suspect a thing, huh?"

Old Blackbeard was on his feet and rushing toward the boys. Blindly, Todd and Buff turned and ran, stumbling, half-falling, pushing through branches and shrubs. Wet weeds and leaves slapped them in the face, but they didn't feel a thing. Old Blackbeard was getting closer.

Buff gasped, "We've got to separate, Todd. I hurt my ankle when I slipped, but he can't catch both of us."

Todd veered off and Old Blackbeard went on after Buff. "Run all you want. We'll get you sooner or later."

Todd was chilled by the words, but he paused just a moment to take stock of where he was. Was it better to keep running? Or hide? He didn't have long to decide, for one of the other men was pounding right after him. Todd spurted on again. He heard a yell and a gasp and he knew that Buff had been captured.

Buff yelled, "Run, Todd, run!" That was the last sound he heard from him.

Todd couldn't turn and help him. His own pursuer was getting closer. Todd knew he must get away and go for help. Only fear and panic kept him going. His body was completely worn out. Up and down hills they scrambled. The man behind him was powerful and grunted with the exertion, but he kept coming. There were only a few yards between them. Todd was desperately trying to think of a maneuver. His heavy rain clothes and boots were holding him back. He just couldn't put on any more speed. If the man got any closer, he decided to hold back a branch from any tree he was passing, to try to knock him back. But how long would that keep him down? He knew that if it ever came to bodily contact, the man would have him in no time.

Seeing a clump of thick alders, Todd dashed into them, stepped back and held a branch. His pursuer plunged after him and, just as Todd was going to release the branch to hit him, he saw the man's face blanch and a look of horror spread over it. Todd had the notion that the man had had a heart attack, or that Todd seemed to him to be a leper or something. What on earth?

The man scudded to a halt as soon as he could, yelled like a maniac, turned, and started wildly back the way he had come. Todd felt the prickles rise on the back of his neck. He forced himself to turn, slowly, again, and look in the direction he had been running. What had the man seen? The fear that had made him run wildly earlier had now given way to paralysis. He could hardly move. Almost as if in a trance, he turned. Somehow he already knew what he would see.

The brownie was standing a few yards ahead of him, on its hind legs. Its giant head was inclined toward him as it either sought to see or smell him or somehow account for the commotion. The massive creature was poised, graceful; and the sheer size, the absolutely incongruous *size* made Todd think of the movies with dinosaurs. Neither Todd nor the bear moved. It was just like a still life. Nearby was a tall, spreading cottonwood. Almost as if it were a rehearsed play and he knew his part well, Todd gently released the alder branch, slowly walked to the cottonwood and began to climb. When he was quite high, he looked out. The bear was still pondering on the little drama. Then he sniffed, turned, and elegantly, disdainfully, loped off. Todd sucked in his breath sharply, seeing how fast the great creature moved. In the back of his mind, he had associated size with slowness and clumsiness, and had felt safer because of it. Now, he saw how wrong he had been.

High in the cottonwood, reality began to penetrate Todd's numbness, and all the *what ifs* began to jump at him. What if the brownie hadn't shown up? What if the brownie had suddenly rushed him? What if – oh, what if the cottonwood hadn't just happened to be there?

With a bit of relaxing over the ordeal, Todd began to feel

very weak, cold and shivery; then very very light-headed. He held tightly to a limb and closed his eyes.

Miserable, he huddled in the tree. What on earth was he to do now? He hadn't the faintest notion where he was. They had run and run and run. They were far, far back in the woods. At this end of the lake, there was better than a hundred miles of wilderness with only a cabin dotted here and there. Buff had told him it was virtually uninhabited. One could wander for days and never stumble upon the houses, nor the tiny little brave roads tracing through the forest. He wasn't even sure which direction they had run. When they started, they were in the general direction of going back home, but that seemed like miles and hours ago. He *had* to get help. Buff was captured. He hadn't any idea what they would do to him, but he doubted if it would be anything that the physiology books would recommend. There was a man looking for him in one direction, and a brownie in another. Oh boy, oh boy. He murmured, "How did I, a city apartment dweller, get into a mess like this?"

For a while, he sympathized with himself and thought of his miseries. He was cold, wet, tired, and now hungry besides. However, he could only stay huddled in a tree so long. Something had to be done. One thing was sure: no help was coming. Buff was captured. His folks were in the hospital. The Jacksons were in Anchorage and wouldn't be back for several days. Even on a long, long shot that his own folks would get worried: they had been sent a letter not to expect any more mail from him for some time. No one was coming. Todd tried to think this out, for in the city, there was always help. There were neighbors, apartment managers, doctors, firemen, police. Here there was nothing – no one but him. Oh boy, he thought, and I'm a fine one for everything to rest on. . . .

He ventured up again and peered out of the tree, trying to see something familiar, something that would tell him where he was. He saw no sign of his pursuer or the bear. There was no sound. Such a nice, peaceful day, just the beauties of Nature. He climbed higher in the tree, trying to see some sign of where the lake was, but all that was visible was more of the same – trees and green hills. Taking one more look to be sure the bear was gone, he climbed cautiously down from the tree and looked around shakily.

Now, I've got to *think,* he said to himself. I've got a knife and some string. I've two candy bars in my pocket. A handkerchief, and, let's see – yep, here's two matches. Darn it, why did Buff have to have the binoculars? I sure could have used them. He looked about. Now what was it I learned in the third grade about being lost in a forest? he asked himself. It had all seemed so unlikely then that it was sort of like guessing at life on Mars. Let's see: does moss grow on the north side of the trees? But even if it does, I don't know what direction I want to go. He sat down to think anew on his problems. What direction was the cabin on the lake? After winding about on the homestead road, he had no idea what direction he was seeking. The sun was no help up here even when it was out; and today it wasn't.

I've got some news for the third-graders, he thought grimly. If they're ever lost up North. . . .

Deciding that he was probably doing the wrong thing, but the only thing he could do under the circumstances, he just started walking – in what he hoped was the direction from which he had come. He tried to be very quiet, on the lookout for the fishermen and bears, and he skirted away very carefully from thick patches of alders or bushes where he couldn't see very far ahead of him, and he kept looking back.

"That much I've learned," he whispered.

At first, he could see some trail where he had run, but in no time, he lost it. Vainly he looked for broken stems or branches or mashed grass and weeds. "Some Indian I am," he said softly. But he was beginning to feel more cheerful. Walking warmed him up. There didn't seem to be a bear about. He was sure just a little walking would take him back to some part of the lake.

He tried to decide upon this path or that, this side of the hill or the other; did he cross that valley, or veer to the right? How alike everything looked! After a good, steady walk, he came to the crest of a hill and climbed another tree. There, dead ahead, was water! It was the lake. Elatedly, he got down, started off again, cautioning himself all the time to be even more careful. The fishermen were somewhere near undoubtedly and looking for him. He stopped every now and then to listen. Another fifteen minutes of walking put him at the water's edge. "All I have to do now is follow the lake shore to the cabin and then follow the road from the cabin out to the Jackson's or someone else." He felt so relieved that he sat down for a minute and ate one of his candy bars. It didn't feel very good on an empty stomach, but he needed more energy.

As he started hiking again, he remembered that he would

soon come to a big swamp, the one they had watched Old Blackbeard cross. But somehow or other, the swamp just didn't show up. He glanced anxiously about the lake. An alarming thought was beginning to cross his mind. Carefully, he examined the pattern of the lake shore, the size of the lake. Oh, if only I'd paid more attention, he worried. Another fifteen minutes of walking, however, convinced him. As if to make it final, he announced to himself, under his breath, "This is a different lake I'm on. I'm really lost now."

He could see no sign of a cabin, road, anything man-made about the lake that would mean inhabitants. There was not a sound to be heard. Even the birds must be keeping themselves dry somewhere. He had never felt more lonesome in his life. Acting on impulse, he blindly started back. He felt he had to go back and start all over. He got to the place where he had sat down to eat the candy. The wrapper was still there. He grabbed it up and put it in his pocket. It had occurred to him that he might need it later. Back he went over the hills. At times it was agonizingly slow as he tried to follow his path or remember how the hills and trees had looked. But finally, he had to admit that, again, he had no idea where he was so far as the cabin was concerned; or Buff's lake, or the lake he had just been on, or the cottonwood the bear had chased him up – or anything that would give him some direction.

"Well, by golly," he decided stubbornly aloud, "one thing I can do. From here on out, I can mark my trail. I don't have to get lost half a dozen times. Once or twice is enough." Deliberately he started breaking weeds; he ripped some bark from birch trees as he walked. Once while he was resting, he pulled his knife out and cut some notches in the trees. He looked constantly for trees with a distinctive shape, something he could remember. He walked and he walked and he walked. In another hour, he again came to a lake—a new one this time. He knew he must be in the wilderness country back of the end of Buff's lake. He recalled Buff's saying that no one lived there and that it was a region with more lakes than Minnesota ever dreamed of.

The sky was a dark, dull gray. He glanced at his watch. It was four-thirty in the afternoon. Carefully, he wound it. It did not need winding but he was very much afraid it just might somehow run down and stop. It was the only contact he had with the measurable realities of time or distance. He sat down at the edge of the lake to rest.

Suddenly there was a crashing in the brush and a movement through the trees. He sat bolt upright. It was only a moose, but just the same, Todd carefully kept behind a tree. Then the huge, ungainly creature walked into the lake and began to dip its head under, coming up with vegetation to eat that it obviously considered choice delicacies. Todd watched with numb interest. He glanced at the sky. It was going to get really dark tonight. The sky looked swollen and sullen. "I'll bet anything it starts to rain again." He had quit thinking his thoughts and was saying them aloud, quietly, but aloud. "Talking to myself already," he muttered wearily. He wondered where Buff was, what they were doing to him. Would they really hurt him? Would they—would they *kill* him? Trying to be realistic about it, he remembered how much Buff said the men had to gain. "I guess people have been killed for lots less than thousands and thousands of dollars."

Spurred on by thinking of Buff's need and trust in him, he got up and started walking again. It was beginning to be an old story: another hour of walking and a brand new lake. "Good grief! All these empty lakes. When I think of all the people back home on little bitty Diamond Lake, or the crowd at the swimming pool. . . ."

Then, he had an idea. "Say, if these lakes have a stream running out of them, like Buff's, then the stream must go somewhere, maybe to the Inlet. I can just follow a stream out. Yeh, sure. I think I even read that in the third grade too." Elatedly, he followed the lake completely around it, and though he found little trickles and streams running down the hills into the lake, he found none running out. He was discouraged. "Well, all right," he said stubbornly, "so that one is a land-locked lake. Maybe the next one won't be." He got up and started plugging away through the woods.

The rain began to come down slowly, softly; but soon it pelted down, drenchingly, endlessly. Todd realized he could walk no longer. He was soaked. He was cold and hungry. He had been walking for six or seven hours. Thoughts of getting out and of helping Buff became secondary and he floundered about for a way to get some rest, to get dry.

He searched, but there was no shelter. No huge rocks such as they had seen near the fish camp. Most of the trees were spruce, slick and wet. He slogged on. It was getting darker. As he went over the top of the next hill, a pretty little lake spread itself out before him. He headed toward it.

Near the bank was a towering, full cottonwood and a

group of birches. "Real trees!" He looked at them thankfully. "I never realized before how nice the real, big, leafy trees are. I'm sick of those evergreens."

When he neared the trees, he saw it was better than he had hoped. Some beavers had been working there and had felled a couple of trees just recently. One of the downed trees had fallen into a limb of the cottonwood and formed a canopy. It was reasonably dry underneath. Thankfully, he crawled in and sank down. For a few moments, he just caught his breath, stretched his tired leg muscles, and rested. Then he took the other candy bar out and ate it, slowly, slowly. He wished he hadn't eaten the other one so fast, and so unappreciatively. But he had been so sure he was just a little way from the cabin.

When the last of the candy bar was gone, he took the two wrappers and carefully put them in his pocket. Then he looked about for some birch bark which Buff had told him burned almost as well as paper. It was all very wet, however. He broke some sticks up into tiny tiny little twigs. All his training and cautioning for as long as he could remember was along the line of preventing forest fires, of all the things *not* to do. Even now, he was feeling a bit apprehensive about trying to start a fire right in the woods. He took his little bundle back under the canopy and pulled the candy wrappers out. He had two matches. Carefully, ever so carefully, he started to strike the first one. It was wet. He had raked it across a small rock and all the tip of the match was scraped off. His heart sank. He picked up the rock and rubbed it dry with his handkerchief. He pulled the other match from his pocket. It was his last hope.

It flipped from his fingers and dropped to the ground. He forced himself to be slow and thorough as he searched for it. It *had* to be right there. Fumbling through the weeds, he found it and held it tight. He looked at it, rubbed it off carefully. He made one last search through all his pockets for any bits of paper or anything that would burn. He had a small handful and he put it with the candy wrappers, the birch bark, and the twigs. Carefully he scratched the match over the rock. It caught, and he put it to the bits of paper. A tiny but cheery flame licked at the paper. The curling edges of the birch bark caught.

How good it looked! He never took his eyes away even as he was searching and feeling about for more little sticks. The fire began to simmer and die down. The sticks were just too wet. Frantically, he dashed out to find more birch bark. It was raining and dark and he couldn't find any very easily. When he did, he ripped great chunks from the tree and rushed back. But it was too late. Only a tiny bit of damp smoke remained of his fire.

He sighed and crawled back into his little hole. "Oh well," he said, "I'll just smell the smoke for a bit; maybe I can convince myself it's a fire."

He scrunched around and made himself as comfortable as he could. Back home he would never have believed he could have gone to sleep under such conditions—lying curled in a circle to keep on dry ground, listening to the rain inches away from him, some of it filtering down through the leaves and landing on his rain clothes. He pulled his hat down over his face and, just before he went to sleep, he said ironically, "One reason I wouldn't have thought I could sleep like this is because I didn't know what it was like to be chased by crooks and brownies and walk for seven straight hours before going to bed. It's amazing what all that will do for you. Right now, I'm just happy to have what I have. I sure hope the beaver doesn't come back after my roof tonight." He began to get drowsy but part of his brain kept cautioning him, "Got to keep one ear cocked for the sound of a bear."

CHAPTER NINE

Todd to the Rescue

Todd awoke frettingly, feeling something wasn't right, or something needed attention. He winced as he stretched his arms and legs. They were stiff from yesterday, they were stiff from sleeping. There was stiffness on top of stiffness in them. The rain had stopped and the air smelled sweet. What had awakened him? What time was it? Cautiously, he crawled out of his hole.

It was still fairly dark. He stumbled down to the lake. There, out of the shadows of the trees, he looked at his watch. It said four-ten. He kneeled down and splashed water on his face. Something still seemed dimly, incessantly trying to get his attention. As he washed his face, his hands paused in midair. He knew what it was! It was the sound of the vehicle he and Buff had heard at the beginning of this whole nightmare!

Prickles began running up and down his back and his face was chilled from the lake water. He shivered from a combination of things. Which direction was the sound coming from? It was first loud, then dim as if the vehicle were going about hills that shut off its noise, or else going through mud or up over hills that put a strain on it and made it louder at times. He walked back up the hill and was almost sure he could place the direction. With a feeling of tremendous relief, he quickly started walking.

Over hills and through valleys, jumping small creeks, Todd went on, the sound getting louder. Soon, to his amazement he was on a road, a trail. He had hit it at right angles and was so unprepared for it that he might have crossed over it. But he paused in the middle and, down to his left, he could see the dark outline of the vehicle. The road was muddy and the going was slow. Should he follow it? He started to, and then was checked by a thought. He was almost sure the camp was in the other direction. The man driving must be going back to the site on the Inlet that he had heard them talking about. Todd turned back and decided to walk a little way just to see if he was right. At lease, he wouldn't get lost any more. However, he had walked only a short distance when he could smell smoke and he knew he was right. His steps quickened.

When he came in view of the camp, he stepped back into the trees. There was no noise. He could make out another vehicle, the one they had seen half-hidden in the bushes. The fire was banked for the night with some big logs. There were some other evidences of people about: tools, rope, and net hanging about, a bench here and there. Suddenly, he heard some scraping and rustling. When it stopped, he peered out again. Then he saw Buff. He was sitting up against a tree and he was twisting and turning, as if trying to stretch or get comfortable. No one else seemed to be around.

Cautiously, Todd crossed the road and crept nearer the camp. He aimed to come up behind Buff and get his attention. When he was within a few yards, he dropped to his hands and knees, crawling through the bushes, pausing every few minutes for any sign that the men were awake, or were hearing him. Inching along, he was soon directly behind Buff's tree. Then he saw that Buff was tied to it. How long had he had to sit there tied to that tree in the rain? Todd was glad he had come back first instead of going the other way down the road.

"Buff!" he whispered hoarsely. "It's me. Are you okay?" He saw Buff start and realized he had been dozing. "Buff! It's me. I'm going to untie you. Don't make any noise."

Quickly, he fumbled in his pocket and found his pocket knife. He sawed on the heavy twine and soon had him cut loose. "My feet. My feet are tied together too."

Todd scrambled over him, and cut his feet loose. Buff was massaging his arms, trying to get more circulation going, loosen them up, and take the stiffness out. They quickly rolled back behind the tree out of the firelight.

Todd rubbed Buff's ankles. "Are you okay? Did they hurt you?"

"No, they didn't hurt me. I haven't been tied so tight very long. Just since they went to bed. But, boy, is that uncomfortable! And am I glad to see you! I sure was worried about you. How did you make out?"

"Maybe I'd better tell you later. We still have to get out of here. Can you walk?"

"I don't know. My feet have been tied up and cramped since this morning, and I sprained my ankle. It sure hurts. I guess that's why Old Blackbeard caught me so easily yesterday. But we can at least hide out in the woods until I can walk, I guess. It's not safe to go home. They're going to start looking for you again in the morning. You know what they're going to do?"

"I give up."

"They're going to dump us in the Inlet – fix it up in a little skiff or something, make it look like an accident. Accidents like that are fairly common in fishing season. The Inlet is so cold that you haven't a chance to swim out."

"Nice people." Todd looked about anxiously. "Are your legs better? How's the ankle? We'd better get out of here. Where are the men?"

"I think they're asleep by now. They crawled into that little box over their pickup bed after Hank took the last load to the beach."

"Yes, I know. That's how I got unlost. I heard the car."

"I wish we had a vehicle."

Without thinking, Todd said, "So do I." But when he looked at Buff, he saw a frown of concentration. "What's up?"

Buff was saying, slowly, "I wonder if we could?"

"Could what?"

"If we could somehow fasten them in that camper thing and drive out of here in it."

"You're kidding! Why, they could get out, couldn't they?"

"Well, there are no windows big enough to get out of. It's just a heavy, homemade wooden box to cover the bed. They could break the lock. It's just a small one on the outside, but if we had a big log chain or something to run around the box, I don't see how they could get out. It's small and cramped. They'll be asleep when we first start and the road will be so bumpy, they'll be mighty uncomfortable and not able to do much. I don't think they have any tools or anything in there."

Todd gulped. "Well, whatever you say, Buff. But we can't fool around. They mean business."

"You telling me? I sat here all tied up listening to them plan how to throw us into the Inlet."

"Well, is there a big chain around?"

"I don't think so. There's one in Hank's rig that they use for pulling and towing, but it isn't big enough to go clear around the box. I know! I know! Listen, Todd, they've got a whole spool of this new nylon rope. It's strong enough to pull the *Queen Mary* in. All the fishermen are using it these days."

"Yes, but a rope might stretch, and if they could stretch it just a little they might be able to bust out. We couldn't tie it tight enough."

"Not this rope. It's different. You remember those little woven Japanese puzzle things we used to put over our finger and the harder we pulled, the tighter it stuck? This rope is like that. They have a little tool to splice it, and when it's spliced, the harder you pull against it, the tighter it gets."

"If you say so, Buff. But, like I said, we can't make any mistakes. We could try to hide you out someplace in the woods if you aren't able to make it in, and I could go for help."

"Yes, we could, but I think that would be just as dangerous. I'm afraid they would find me – or you. You'd have to get past Hank down at the site. You see, he has a real, legitimate site and he sells all these fish as if he caught them there. I wondered how they sold them from back here to the canneries, because the canneries know every fishing site and every boat out there. I'll bet they think his site is really going to town this year!"

Buff started to rise, but his ankle gave way and, from the expression on his face, Todd knew he was in great pain. He whispered, "Okay, Buff, we'll try it your way. You tell me where that rope is and I'll get it."

"It's right across the road there where you see that pile of net and stuff. Right in the top of it, they stuck this blue plastic splicer. It's not much bigger than a table knife but it's hollow – like a fountain pen. You'll know it when you see it. Just bring it to me and I'll figure out how to do it."

Carefully, Todd tiptoed through the woods, across the road, and to the pile of gear. The spool was heavy. He found the splicer right there, too, stuck it in his pocket, and picked up the spool. He was weak from hunger and nervousness, but he lugged it to Buff.

Buff began uncoiling rope. "What we've got to do is have everything ready and do it all quick. We'll take this next to the truck. You run it around the box and as soon as it goes clear around, I'll cut and splice it. You lock the door. It's just a little padlock. It's swinging loose; just fasten it. Then we get in and drive away. Can you drive, Todd?"

"Sure, school driving-lesson style."

"Good. I'm not sure I have enough steam in this foot to drive. But forget most of what they told you in school. The rougher you make this drive, the better. I can hang on, but the more they're bumped about, the less thinking they can do. Have you ever driven a truck or anything with a gear shift?"

"Only a couple of times, but we'll manage. From the sound of that rig of Hank's, he's driving in low all the way in the mud."

"Good. I can help you." Buff pulled himself up and, dragging his bad foot, scooted toward the truck. He had cut off enough rope so he wouldn't have to handle the spool. He cut it plenty long so there would be more than enough to go around once. Todd took one end of it and went the other way about the truck.

Todd's heart was pounding. How much noise were they making? How soundly did Old Blackbeard sleep? Stealthily, he walked around the truck. Once he scraped against something and caught his coat. With shaking fingers, he loosened it.

It had seemed miles, but finally, finally, he handed his end to Buff, who was leaning against the back fender. Quickly, Buff cut the extra rope off, and spliced it. With the rope that was left, he made a little loop, put a stick in it and twisted it about the rope to tighten it very tight. With hands shaking, Todd reached over, within just inches of where the sleeping men lay behind the camper's doors, probably within four inches of a heavy foot, and clicked the padlock into place.

Buff whispered, "No use waking them up before we have to. Let's get in real easy. Now, this truck – you have to push down on the starter. It's on the floorboard, but it starts easy. They used it today."

Carefully, they opened their doors and slid into the seat. Buff leaned over and silently pointed out the mechanics to Todd, who nodded. There was still no sound from the men.

Todd turned the key, paused, then resolutely pressed down on the starter. Buff's eyes were glued to him, ready to help with his hands or his left foot. The engine kicked over, spat, sputtered, and died. "Again," called Buff. Todd did so and this time, as it caught, Buff quickly hit the accelerator with his left foot. The truck roared and so did the men in the back.

"Push the clutch in!" Buff cried. "Let's go!" As Todd pushed the clutch in, Buff pulled the gear into reverse. They backed into the brush. "Now, again, and I'll put it in low for you."

"Okay, Todd?"

Todd nodded. Away they went. "I'll make it there one way or another." Anxiously, he asked, "Can you tell what they're doing? How does it sound?"

Buff grinned. "It sounds bumpy back there."

"I was beginning to wonder if they were even in there, it took so long for them to wake up."

"They were there. I wouldn't have made a mistake like

that. But they were dead tired. They've been picking and loading fish all day and all night. They had to get them out to Hank's site in time for this fishing period and it starts at six this morning. It must be almost that by now. Oh yes, and they had to chase us. That took a lot of energy."

"Buff, just in case they *do* get out, what do we do?"

"You just keep driving as fast as you can. If they jump out, it will take them a minute to get to their feet. Unless we run into a stump or mudhole, we can surely drive faster than they can run. But if they do jump on, just keep going. I'll try to knock them off, or hit them with something. The best weapon we have is this car."

Todd gulped. He was dog-tired and hungry but on razor's edge. The thumping of the men sounded like it was right on the back of his neck by now. He had never seen such a road in his life. It was, at the most optimistic level, only a rude trail. There were sticks and stumps and branches that scraped. There was barely room to squeeze through most of the time. The ruts were horrible. He could feel one wheel settle down with a thud while another one was trying to climb a rise. The main track was slick and slippery with mud. There were places where it just dropped off into a little pool of water. Once he started to hesitate and decide the best route, but Buff shouted, "Don't stop! Hit it with all you got." The pickup roared, floundered, bounced, but ground through.

Buff grinned. "I'll give you an A in your Alaska driving lesson. Good thing we got a pickup with a box on it and a couple of heavy prisoners. It probably wouldn't pull these mudholes without that weight on the back."

It seemed to Todd he had spent most of his life driving this road. His arms clenched the wheel which continually seemed to jump away from him. His eyes ached from straining to see the road, gauge distances between stumps, judge the degree of mud and holes. Buff stuck his head out his window from time to time to see if there was anyone crashing out of the box. But it seemed to him that it was quieter back there than it was at first. Were they methodically working out a means of escape?

"Buff, do you know how long this road is?"

"Not for sure. It *can't* be as long as it seems. We just don't have roads that long. Now, when we come out, I think we'll drive right down onto the beach. There are two things to watch out for and one is Hank. He probably won't notice anything at first, but, if he does, look out. Maybe, though, he'll be busy fishing or getting ready to fish and we can just drive right on by. The surf makes a lot of noise. The other thing to watch is not to get stuck in the sand. Just give it all its got. We'll keep going until the road goes back up to the main highway, or until we see some help. Stay close to the water; the sand is usually harder-packed there."

Todd listened carefully. Was there a new challenge around every corner? A new fear?

"Todd, have you got your watch on? If it's six or after, Hank will be fishing."

"I've got it on, but I can't look at it and watch this road. I've been winding it every few hours. I was afraid it would run down out in the woods. Maybe I can get it off and you can see it."

"Don't do it if it bothers. We'll know soon enough anyway. Whatever time it is or whatever Hank's doing, we'll just have to get by him if we can."

Buff had hardly finished saying that when the road opened up and the beach was below them. It was brighter and sunnier out of the trees. There was water stretching before them. All in a single, quick impression, Todd saw the sand, the water, a few boats that looked like specks on the horizon and white seagulls diving and careening. It was all there, just like a picture postcard. "Except picture postcards don't show people crashing through sand with a load of crooks while trying to get by another crook."

Buff looked anxiously at Todd. "Are you all right? You look a little pale. Just hang on a little longer and really hit it now."

The minute the pickup rolled onto the sand, Todd could feel the difference: it settled, dug in, and slowed to a grinding growl. No slippery trail here. It frightened him. They were almost to a stop. He was doing something wrong.

Buff was yelling encouragement. "You're doing just fine. Follow the track. You're doing great. This old rig has a lot of power. Soon as we get out on the beach farther, the sand will get harder and it will be easier. It's deepest and softest here."

Heartened, Todd applied himself and squinted at the sudden, surprising glare of sun on sand. There was a little black tarpaper shack ahead of them with fishing and living essentials strewn about.

Buff shouted, "That's Hank's place! Try to turn it to the left. Let's try to miss him by several yards. If he does see us, he won't have time to do anything about it. One thing about being here, the noise of the surf will give us a break."

Todd turned the pickup but just that much angle of the tires halted it, and the pickup lurched and died sickeningly.

"Start it up, start it up! We're not really stuck. Just straighten your wheels out. We won't turn there." Buff was already out and, as Todd started the truck, he pushed with all his might on his side. The truck moved forward and he hopped in on his good foot. He rubbed the other one.

"Does it hurt bad, Buff?"

"I sure couldn't run any races. Look, let's not chance getting stuck again. We're *so* close. Just drive right past Hank and follow his trail on up the beach. If we can get to the other side of his cabin, the sand should be good and hard."

But their one little fiasco had already alerted Hank and, as the boys pulled the pickup around the corner of his cabin, his vehicle suddenly darted toward them and rather than crash head-on, Todd instinctively slammed on the brakes. Hank leaped from his truck.

"Start up again, Todd! Back up! Do anything!"

Frantically, Todd started the truck, backed up, tried to evade Hank. He started forward, driving at an angle to miss the rig that blocked his path. Hank leaped on the front of the truck. They weren't going fast and Todd could see nothing but the man on the hood. He drove blindly.

Hank crawled up to the windshield. He was shouting something. Todd's door had no window in it and Hank's huge hand was reaching in, grabbing for the steering wheel,

for Todd. To Todd, it was like the horror movies he had seen as a kid: the monster closing in and getting closer. The great hand moving in. It was hard to believe, too, that he should evade or hurt or run counter to an adult. Always before, he was taught to do what adults said, to try to please. The black, hairy hand grabbed the steering wheel and Todd and Buff wrenched at it while the truck lurched crazily here and there in the sand. Hank was leaning way over the front and would soon be able to come in the window right on Todd.

From somewhere, Todd heard Buff's voice saying calmly, "I've got the steering wheel, Todd. I've got it. Here, use this. Keep going. Don't let up on the gas."

As if in a dream, Todd gazed down at his hand where Buff had pressed a cold rusty monkey wrench. It looked vaguely familiar. Stupidly, he looked at it.

"Use it, Todd! Use it!"

As the great, mean, red face of Hank was almost in the window, Todd raised the wrench, closed his eyes, and brought it down. He felt the steering wheel jerk free and felt Buff pulling the truck to the right. He heard Hank fall. He opened his eyes. Ahead was a bright, sunny beach. He put his hand on the wheel. "I've got it!" He leaned out the window and looked back. Hank lay prone on the sand.

"Can we just leave him there? What if I killed him?"

"Keep going. Yes, we can leave him there. We'll be back in no time now with help. Probably the next site or two will have someone there who will help us. No, you didn't kill him. You hardly touched him. I'm surprised it even knocked him off, but it did."

Todd drove on down the unbelievable beach with its unbelievable history. Dimly he saw Buff swing his binoculars out from under the raincoat that he still wore and look closely at the next settlement on the beach that meant another site and another family.

"Oh, Todd! It's over, it's all right. I know these people! We're going to make it!"

Todd remembered braking the pickup right at the shack and turning off the key. He remembered Buff's jumping out, and hopping and dragging his leg, running and calling. He remembered seeing surprised but kind faces look up. And that's all he remembered. He had just opened the door, gotten out, and then keeled over in the early morning coolness on the sand.

When he came to, he was on a little cot in a frame shack: a one-room affair that was a marvel of efficiency. Everything one would need from an egg turner to band-aids seemed to line the walls. Shelves were built of wooden crates. He heard people talking and a man was saying, "Just spoils it for everyone. Can't be too rough on fellers like that. I *wondered* how in the world Hank was hittin' so good up on that site this year when we weren't. I saw them fish trucks go by time and again, loaded down."

Todd sat up. "What's happening?"

People looked up at him. Buff smiled. "Okay now, Todd? Everything is just fine. Tom, here, had a radio and he called for help. A State Patrol and a Fish and Game man are both on their way. Be just a little bit yet. Tom's son is guarding the truck. I guess we banged our passengers up a bit. They don't seem to have much life."

"What about Hank? Did I kill him?"

Tom laughed and slapped a knee. "Kill him? He was up and starting to come after you in a minute. But we took care of him too." He gave a great guffaw. "Why, Hank's been hit harder than that with bottles in bars and thought he was havin' fun. You just threw him off the truck."

Todd sighed and leaned back. "I never want to see another monkey wrench as long as I live." He could still feel the thump as he had brought it across Hank's skull.

A heavy-set, motherly-looking woman labored up the steep stairs into the shack that was perched up on piling. She clucked at him and Buff. "Bless your hearts. Such brave boys. How about some bacon and eggs?" She was wearing jeans like all the other women he had seen in Alaska, but Todd thought he had never seen a more enchanting lady.

"Oh, thank you, ma'am," Todd answered. "I'm so hungry I can eat them shells and all. I think that's why I passed out. I'm so sorry. But when I saw the brownie, it made me so weak, and all I've had since is a can –"

"Brownie? What brownie? You saw a brownie?"

"You remember, Buff. I told you, or maybe I didn't, that a brownie kept that guy from catching me – oh well, I'll not bore you with that now."

"Bore us? Why bear stories make you famous around here, and now you have one!" Buff looked about at the others. "What do you think of this city dude that comes up here and catches crooks, has a run-in with a bear. . . ."

The lady looked at Todd fondly. "Well, I think he's really something, that's what I think." Todd felt a warm glow at her kind words. She passed out plates with delicious food that, seemingly, she had magically concocted in just seconds. Todd decided that this was one type of woman very often overlooked and underappreciated in our society. "This is just wonderful," he told her.

She smiled and handed a plate to Buff. "How are your folks, Buff?"

As the boys ate and they all visited, she fixed Buff's ankle. Tom Larson stood up. "Well, Mother, it looks like you can handle our friends here. The fish period opens pretty quick. I'd better get busy." He had just stepped outside, when he stuck his head back in. "Here's the State Patrol and the Fish and Game is right behind him. As soon as you boys get finished, come on out, okay?"

CHAPTER TEN

Fame, Fortune, and Loon Lake

It was much, much later that the boys were in town in the magistrate's office that served as a courtroom, and in the company of the officers and three prisoners. A special magistrate had been summoned and flown in from Anchorage, and the newspaper had sent down a reporter, for the tale of the two daring boys had trickled through.

The local magistrate had been looking fixedly, as if puzzled, at Hank's two fellow prisoners. "Just a minute," he said to everyone. "I have a feeling I've seen them somewhere before, even if they do say they just came to Alaska." He went to his cabinets and pulled out the folder of pictures of wanted criminals that the FBI and various agencies sent him. Suddenly, he straightened, "Well, well, well, well."

He held up the folders, and looked at Todd and Buff.

"Boys, it looks like you picked yourselves a couple of winners." He idly read part of the captions under the pictures: ". . . armed robbery, suspicion of murder . . . considered dangerous. . . ." He paused a moment and then went on: ". . . $10,000.00 reward leading to the capture and arrest –"

His last words were lost in the uproar in the little office. Flash bulbs popped as the newspaperman began taking pictures of the two dazed boys. The magistrate continued humorously, "I believe everyone would agree that this leads to the capture and arrest."

The reporter was shooting questions at them right and left. Some excited onlookers bolted for the door, to tell the townsfolk. Ten thousand dollars!

"Mom." Buff said, "I've got to tell Mom and Dad. Todd! Do you know what this will mean? Why, my half of the reward will be five thousand dollars! That's more than Dad could have made working this year. It will be tight, but maybe we can save the homestead after all."

The reporter picked up his ears at this and, little by little, the whole tale came out about the homestead and Buff's parents, who were in the hospital; then the whole adventure from start to finish, including Todd's encounter with a brownie. More flash bulbs popped and then the newspaperman jumped up. "Got to get on that plane. Got to hit the next edition."

The police were taking the prisoners away. Gradually the first crowd ebbed away and was replaced by a new one: friends who had just heard the terrific news. The magistrate was saying to the boys, "Well, I suppose those fellows just figured Alaska was far enough away so that no one would

ANTED!
10,000
REWARD
REWA

ever find them, a good place to hide out. I'm glad we caught them for lots of reasons, and one is the fine pure and simple. I can't see why Hank ever got tied up with them, though. He's lived here long enough to hate that kind of thing too. He knows it's hurting the whole fishing industry." He sighed. "I suppose people just get greedy."

Buff and Todd started out through the throng. They were heroes. There was nothing too good for them. No one would hear of their going home. They had to stay in town. Tomorrow night there was to be a town meeting. The magistrate would make an official announcement about the reward money. There would be a band. The fishing period was over for a couple of days and the fishermen would be in.

The two days seemed to whirl by. The boys told their story over so many times, it began to sound like a record. Buff nudged Todd happily. "How do you like being a celebrity?"

Todd grinned, "Believe me, you're talking to someone who has all his life been just as far from the limelight as one can get. But it's kind of fun, isn't it?"

Buff had called his mother and found that they were coming home in a couple of days. "Buff, we've seen the papers. Your pictures are a foot high. You'll get the papers down there today probably. We're so proud now that it's over. But we'd have been scared stiff if we had known what was going on."

Then the boys were back at the lake, reading the write-ups for the fifty-sixth time. Todd said, "They'll never believe it. They'll just never believe it when I tell them."

"Who won't?"

"Dad, Mother, Jamey—anyone who's ever known me. I think I could have won hands down a title like 'Least likely to receive fame and fortune;' or 'Least likely to become involved in capturing crooks' – that, for sure – what's the matter?"

Buff struck his hand on his head and jumped to his feet. "My gosh, Todd," he said, "I'm sorry. Everything was in such a rush and everyone was talking at once, and he just handed this to me and said to give it to you, and I couldn't get to you right then and –"

Todd looked at him curiously. "What *are* you talking about?"

Buff was frantically searching through his pockets. "The telegram. You got a telegram . . . here." He handed a crinkled-up envelope to Todd, and watched as Todd tore it open. He saw the amazement in Todd's face. "Well, what does it say? Is it secret?"

Todd's voice was thick and his hands trembled. He gulped when he tried to talk. It says, "Picture and story of you made all our papers. So proud we're about to bust. Can't wait to hear from you. All our love. Dad, Mother, and Jamey."

Buff yelped and pounded Todd on the back. "*How about that?* The papers way back there! We're famous! I'll bet your Dad really is proud of you too!" He continued talking happily and tried to ignore the suspicious little drops of moisture in the corner of Todd's eyes.

"Yes," Todd said slowly, as if he were letting it seep

through him, word by word, "yes, Dad is proud of me – finally."

"Oh, Todd, I'll bet he's always been proud of you. You just haven't listened at the right times."

Todd looked at Buff for a moment, then said, "You know, you may be right. It's just that Jamey was always so good at the things Dad liked and, gee, it bothered me. But, after the things that have happened up here, a little game of tennis doesn't seem quite so important. It's a *big* world, isn't it? With lots of things in it. I guess we shouldn't get in such a rut. And, you know, I guess Dad was proud of the ribbon I won in the speech contest. Maybe as proud as he *could* be, maybe as proud as *I'll* be able to be if my son makes a touchdown. Maybe I'll just let Jamey make the touchdowns from now on and not worry about it."

"Atta boy, and *you* can take care of the crooks and bears. Fifty-fifty."

Todd grinned, then feinted with a left hook at Buff. "You nut," he said, but golly, it did sound good! "I'll take care of the crooks and bears."

They relaxed happily, resting up over the excitement. A soft breeze rippled the sunny waves of the lake and the loon called from his corner.

Todd said slowly, "This is the swellest place I've ever seen. It's the home that I'll have inside me from now on. I'll always have it now even when I'm back in the city."

"Yes, just barely. Thanks to robbers and rewards."

"Silly. I didn't mean I'd actually have it. I just meant it will be my retreat when I'm back in the apartment and need to get away. I'll just close my eyes and imagine I'm here and listening to that crazy loon. But that reminds me, Buff, you said something about your half of the reward. You can have it all. I don't want any of it."

Buff looked up. "Are you nuts? You don't want five thousand dollars! Why, you *earned* it. You really earned all of it. If it hadn't been for you, not only would those guys not have been captured but I'd be at the bottom of the Inlet right now."

"That hasn't anything to do with it. Five thousand won't put you in the clear on the homestead and give you anything to live on this coming year. You'll have hospital bills for your folks. You need the whole ten."

"I don't care what we need; that's yours, fair and square."

"Buff, believe me, I don't need the money. My dad makes plenty. He's not rich, but he makes plenty. He already has an insurance policy nearly paid up to put Jamey and me through college. And I know how much a few thousand means to you. Now this is where I'm right and you've been wrong: remember I told you that you were in a rut about how hard money was to come by. See? I was right. There are ways. There's ten thousand dollars you never dreamed of."

Buff laughed. "You're right. I never once thought of capturing crooks to make enough to get the field cleared. But, still –"

Todd stopped him. "I'm not fooling. Just call me a good paying guest if you want. Or – Dad is always telling us about investments. Let's just pretend a hunk of the homestead is mine — whatever you want; but keep the ten thousand. There's nothing I'd rather see five thousand spent on than this place. I just think I'll come back next year."

The full implication was just beginning to dawn on Buff. "You really are serious, aren't you? Why, with ten thousand dollars — why, Todd, that ought to do it: finish the clearing and planting, pay the hospital bills, and buy winter's groceries. Maybe even enough for some livestock." Buff's eyes were beginning to glow and, excitedly, the boys began planning. "Oh, just wait 'til Dad and Mom hear of this!"

Todd suddenly said, "Oh, I guess I will take a couple of dollars out of that ten thousand."

Buff grinned. "A couple of dollars? Sure, but what for?"

Todd patted the papers with the inch-tall headlines and the huge pictures of them. "Oh, I just might want to invest in the newspaper game — say fifty copies or so for keepsakes."

Buff laughed. "I guess we both got what we wanted and needed out of this."

"Yes, and Hank and Old Blackbeard and their friend got what they needed."

The boys began to laugh at the shared memory, now that it was all safely behind them.

"And you'll really come back next year, Todd?"

"You couldn't keep me away with a monkey wrench."